THE HOME STRETCH

BOOKS BY WAYNE M. JOHNSTON

The Home Stretch
North Fork

THE HOME STRETCH

Wayne M. Johnston

Black Heron Press
Post Office Box 614
Anacortes, Washington 98221
www.blackheronpress.com

The Home Stretch is a work of fiction. All characters that appear in this book are a product of the author's imagination. Any resemblance to persons living or dead is entirely coincidental.

Mr. Johnston would like to thank the colleagues, friends, and family members who read the several drafts of this book and offered encouragement, with special thanks to his publisher, Jerry Gold, whose guidance and support have been invaluable.

ISBN (print): 978-1-93636434-3
ISBN (ebook): 978-1-936364-35-2

Black Heron Press
Post Office Box 614
Anacortes, Washington 98221
www.blackheronpress.com

For Bill and Judy Matchett

All that breathe
Will share thy destiny
So live, that when thy summons comes
Approach thy grave
Like one who wraps the drapery of his couch
About him, and lies down to pleasant dreams.

—from "Thanatopsis" by William Cullen Bryant

One

It's a lovely afternoon in late spring. Sun. Calm, sparkling water spans the breadth of Saratoga Passage. A distant sailboat, tiny from where we sit on Whidbey Island, heads north along Camano shore.

"So, when's your last day?"

High tide covers the expansive mud flat beyond the cement bulkhead that protects the front of the cabin from winter storms. This place is full of memories for me, punctuating the passage of decades. It has evolved since the days of no neighbors and the decaying travel trailer my friend, Ben, put here to sleep in when he first bought the lot. When he could afford it, he built a small cabin. Later, he expanded it into what now is still a cabin, but big enough to accommodate overnight family get-togethers with grown kids and their kids.

A rebuilt deck is the most recent change. It's much bigger than what it replaced and it transforms the space between the house and the bulkhead, conforming to what has become a gated community of upscale summer homes. He's finished telling me the story, first about the old bench collapsing, making it clear that it was time, then about finding the right person to rebuild. I don't remember how the connection was made, but the guy was experienced, reasonable about price, and struggling to make a go of it here in America, probably undocumented. For both of us, the struggle to make a go of it is over. I'm retired from teaching high school English, my second career. Ben is about to retire.

It's a big move.

Our work becomes what defines us and it's an ongoing trade, time for money. Even those of us who have had the good fortune of doing things we love end up having the way we work dictated by other people's visions, and when life is difficult, the dream of retirement is a safety valve giving us hope. Our time will finally be our own, safe from the compromise and indignity of the struggle.

"It'll be at least the end of August," he answers. "I'm negotiating a severance package."

Time for money. For several years now, a job that once offered a challenge and a good income has made him miserable, so that he has to be careful navigating his departure, suppressing the urge to speak his mind. He's slipped a few times. Emails intended for a trusted colleague have ended up in the wrong hands and he's had to apologize, playing the crusty old guy card.

"You know this doesn't end well," he says.

"Meaning?"

"You've seen it. We've all seen it. There's no escaping it. We're on our way out. The best we can do is to try and preserve a little self-respect."

Most of us hang on to denial as long as we can, assuming we'll live until at least eighty. The process of retiring puts the numbers in front of us and makes us confront our mortality. Who will outlive whom? Is taking the lower retirement pay to give your spouse survivorship the right choice? Decline, both physical and in status, goes hand in hand with no longer being in the race.

We've both had to settle estates, be executors, sort through and clean up, deal with decline, then the absence of others. His parents are dead. My wife's parents are gone, and so are mine. Most recently for Ben, it was an uncle he was fond of. After a battle that lasted several years, breast cancer defeated my mother. My father's last years were anything but dignified.

When I was forty-three, I put my father in a nursing home. Later the same week I was diagnosed with leukemia. Since then, my life has been a series of extensions, but it started feeling that way long before.

Two

The wedding happened way too soon, and when my father asked me to be best man, I struggled. He was marrying a woman he had worked with for years and who had been part of our lives for as long as I could remember. My mother knew it would happen and said as much shortly before she died at age sixty-two. That my father would ask me to stand with him was a surprise, a shock. We had long been each other's nemesis and the request showed I had gained his respect. That mattered to me, so I accepted. It was a difficult day. Except for a few funerals and weddings, I hadn't been inside a church since I took a stand at age fifteen and refused to attend.

The ceremony was over. I found a quiet moment in the empty bathroom away from the reception and was drying my hands at one of those cloth-towel-loop contraptions. Two men came through the door, my father's friends from Gethsemane, faces from my childhood, somewhat aged. Faces I'd rather have avoided.

"You're Bill," one of the men said.

"Yes."

They introduced themselves, unnecessarily. I knew who they were. It was awkward. I was the disgrace, the source of my parents' grief, the troubled kid they'd heard about and prayed for in prayer meetings. One of them said,

"I hear you work on a tugboat."

"Yeah," I said.

"That must be some life. Your dad's really proud of you."

Three
February, 1985

I first met the Pacific Ocean at Cannon Beach, Oregon when I was a kid. Tourists hadn't taken over the town yet and we had the beach to ourselves. The sense of amazement, the size and power of all that water, the sound of it breaking on the rocks and miles of flat sand has stuck with me. I felt puny at the edge of the vastness. It was like looking into space, at the moon and stars. That sense of awe seems universal. The seashore draws crowds. It can be calming and it inspires hope that, in spite of whatever it's like where you are, there are new places, possibilities on the other side.

Then you find yourself out in it, beyond the surf, grown up.

I'm in the engine room of a tugboat. We're about thirty-five miles offshore between Cape Flattery and the mouth of the Columbia River. Later today, we'll pass Cannon Beach. In this weather there's no place to hide. The entrances to safe harbors are not accessible. I'm the boat's immune system, chief engineer, chief antibody. Essentially the boat is a floating robot controlled from the pilothouse by three small levers. It's my job to know the machinery and the interdependent hydraulic, pneumatic and electrical systems and keep it all working. I also have an Operator's License. We're trailing a quarter-mile of steel cable connected to a cargo barge, a giant floating box, packed tight with rolls of newsprint from a mill in Canada, destined for California newspapers.

The cool steel of the bulkhead separating the engine room from a fuel tank is my backrest. I can feel the boat climb each swell and drop into the trough. It's hard to stand, so I'm sitting on a five-gallon, bilge-soap bucket. I've turned up the flow rate of the centrifuge that cleans fuel as it's transferred from storage tanks to the day tank that the engines draw from. I've also adjusted the desalinator converting seawater to potable water to keep pace with our use. My inspection of gauges and bilges is complete. Everything is as it should be.

During the night, south of Cape Flattery, we hit seas sixty feet or better. It's hard to tell in the dark. We had to slow down. At times we were blown backwards into the open sea behind us. The worst of it has passed. Everything held together and now we're making headway.

As engine rooms go, this one is spacious and bright, polished aluminum diamond-plate decks, white bulkheads, spotless engines. Even the overhead beams, the hull frames and the inside surface of the steel plating that separates this space from the ocean are freshly painted, white, clean. Since it's below the center of gravity and slightly aft of center, where I'm sitting is probably the most stable place on the boat, least affected by the rough sea, but the foam plugs in my ears and the headphones over them only take the edge off the deafening scream of the engines.

The propulsion engines are not yet at full operating speed. It's still too rough. The symmetrical layout of the clean space before me would inspire confidence except for the built-in flaw of the engines. They're light-weight, high RPM, turbo-charged sixteen-cylinder diesels. At full RPM they each deliver 1,200 horsepower, but we never max them out. They feel like hotrod engines and wrong for the job they are doing. To save money, when the boat was built, they were adapted for marine use, converted from hospital backup-generator power plants. They were designed for intermittent emergency use rather than longevity. The company that built the boat got what they paid for, and now we get to live with it.

Out here where dependability matters, they're worrisome. That there are two helps. We rebuild them often. When one fails—and it is *when, not if*—at least there's a backup to keep you pointed in the right direction, alive, while you make repairs, or until help comes. The two smaller generator engines forward of the main engines are run alternately to power the boat's electrical equipment. They are very dependable, but can't make the propellers turn.

Above the big electrical panel that stands between the propulsion engines and divides the engine room, there are stored boxes containing spare air filters. A loose tag of brown paper tape on the end of one whips in the constant blast of air pumped through a duct from outside. Otherwise there's no motion to see, belying what's actually going on, the frantic fragility of stressed pistons, bearings and gears, hidden by spotless engine paint inside those inert shapes. When up to speed, the passive-looking machines burn a hundred gallons of diesel fuel an hour. The dollar amount on the slip I sign after each fueling would easily pay off the mortgage on my house.

Except for the engine room and a small space that houses the steering hydraulics above the rudders, the hull below the deck is fuel tank, water tank, or ballast tank. The boat rides best when low in the water, so as we burn fuel we take on seawater ballast, and as we use potable water, we desalinate seawater to replace it. This boat is slightly bigger than those Columbus sailed or those that brought the first colonists, but by today's standards, it's a very small ship. The colonists didn't fill the hulls with diesel fuel and tow huge barges.

I take another tour of my gauges before going up the ladder.

The captain is perched in the pedestal chair, alone in the pilothouse. His feet straddle the compass on the dashboard. Occasionally the radio squawks with static, but even the bottom-fishermen that sweep the continental shelf with trawl nets and sell to Russian factory ships are quiet this morning. I sit on the bench by the chart table. Neither of us has slept much.

"Everything okay down there?" the captain asks.

I nod. He yawns and continues.

"Get any sleep last night?"

"Dozed a little." I say, "You?"

"No. Got to worrying," he says. "I'm not sure we got the air bags right in the bow of the barge. The office claims damage is killing them."

"We'll find out when we get there." I say. "Can't do anything about it now. If you want to lie down, I've got it for a while."

Even though the swells have dropped, they're still more than a third of the length of the boat, thirty-five feet, give or take. The windows are hit with blasts as though from a fire hose as the wind whips the tops off the waves and picks up our bow spray. When I'm alone, I dig out a cassette tape from a case I keep in one of the cupboards. Vivaldi Concertos, the really busy string ones. I set the volume loud enough to drown the engine noise without bothering the guys sleeping, and perch in the big chair.

Whatever it was that Vivaldi was trying to reflect had to feel something like it does to be in this chair right now. Powerful string instruments, lots of energy and depth, a boldness that fits the dance we're doing. There's sadness and danger in it too. It's a good soundtrack for a great ride. This is the ocean, better than a mechanical bull or a rollercoaster. Everything is gray or foamy and the music is just right as the boat climbs each swell and drops into the trough.

I lose the mood before Vivaldi is played out. The tape lasts about forty-five minutes. Imagine being stuck on a roller coaster for days. It's hard to sustain any kind of adrenalin rush for long, trapped in a noisy box that's being relentlessly battered. When the weather is good, it's like a desert out here, miles and miles of nothing. An occasional albatross skims the crests, seagulls cluster over schools of small fish. Farther south, brown pelicans show up. Dolphins sometimes surround us, several airborne at once, breaking the monotony. Mostly it's gray and lonely and empty.

On one of my first ocean trips, there was a full moon and clear sky. I got a blanket, put on my insulated coveralls and lay aft of the pilothouse, on the upper deck, just taking it in. Another time, different boat, I had to climb the wooden mast at night to change a running-light bulb. The weather wasn't as nasty as today, but there was enough swell that I had to cling tightly to the swaying pole. The boat felt small under me. The ocean was endless, validating my sense of isolation and insignificance.

When we're off Cannon Beach, I remember my daughter's birthday. I reserve calls home on the marine radio for special occasions like this. They're expensive and the connection can be unsatisfying. It's a party line. Anyone within range who wants to relieve boredom can listen in. I've heard some interesting conversations.

After five rings my wife answers. There's commotion and kid noise in the background. Birthday party, seven-year-old girls. I say where we are and try to predict when we'll arrive in Long Beach; then my daughter is given the phone.

"Hi, Daddy."

"Happy Birthday."

"When are you coming home?"

"Pretty soon. Who's at your party?'

"You know, my friends. Gotta go. See you when you come home. Bye."

As the receiver clicks and the connection breaks, another big gusher comes over the bow and slams the pilothouse. I'm ready for calm now, but according to the weather report, it's not likely to come until we get halfway down the California coast. At the four to five knots we're making between storms, it could take days. I'll try to keep the voice connection with my family and the short rush of Vivaldi euphoria present in my mind.

Four
1993

The French doors that separate the family room from the kitchen are closed, but I can hear if he gets up. He had a restless night. Finally he went to sleep and was sleeping soundly on the hide-a-bed while my wife and kids managed to get off to work and school. I'm taking advantage of the quiet, trying to prepare myself for the day by meditating on the couch in the living room, which is where I sleep when he's here.

My body is starting to let go when I hear movement. My heart rate takes off and I'm on my feet, scrambling for the kitchen. I see him through the door glass, struggling with the knob in the half-light. When he sees me he seems glad and calls me by my dead uncle's name. I step in something wet on the floor. There's a puddle under and around the big wood rocking chair we bought when my daughter was born, to rock her back to sleep after night feedings. The sheepskin pad on the seat has a big yellow splotch.

"Did you pee on the chair?" blurts out of me.

"I used the urinal."

It's clear he has no idea what he's done and likely would have done it even if I had remembered to reopen one of the French doors after the family left. I pour him a cup of coffee and get him settled at the kitchen table with one of the bakery donuts I bought him yesterday. He stays occupied long enough for me to change my socks and clean up the pee.

Before I cook him breakfast, I have him "help" me fold up the hide-a-bed. He again refers to me by his older brother's name. I get brave and ask him about his son. Me.

"He made a big mistake about the truck."

"What truck?"

"There was a good deal on a truck that he needed. He should have bought it, but he was stubborn and kept the wrong one."

He's talking about the pickup he spent too much money on and tried to sell to me. I say, "Maybe he liked the one he already had."

"There was a lot of trouble with him. His house was near the university and he got involved with the wrong people. His house was called Bill's Den of Iniquity, and I had to keep the other kids from going there. He sold drugs."

"He always seemed like a pretty good kid to me."

"When judgment comes, I'll stand up for the Lord. They'll want to know whose side you're on."

I know where this is likely to go and am relieved that the phone rings. The woman's voice on the line is formal and asks me to confirm that she's speaking to Bill Smith. She identifies herself as representing the nursing home at Ascension Ministries. In one of his lucid moments earlier in the progression of the disease, he told me it was where he wanted to go when the time came. It's a good nursing home, expensive, and even though he's connected there, we've been on the waiting list for a year.

The woman on the phone is telling me that there is a bed available. If we don't take it, we wait until another spot opens, which I know means until an Alzheimer's patient dies. She gives me until the end of the business day to decide. I look at the rocking chair, now smelling of Lysol and bare of the urine-soaked sheepskin. It takes about fifteen minutes to make the necessary calls to family members. The nursing home will be a big expense, but I won't have to bear it alone and there's the option of selling his property.

We've managed to delay this decision for the eighteen months since he became too much for his wife to handle. My brother, Daniel, took leave from his job to be the primary caregiver. He and Dad sleep in an Airstream trailer parked next to Daniel's house. Daniel sleeps on the couch, doing guard duty by the door to keep Dad from wandering off at night.

Daniel has small children, and the toll it's taking on his family is clear, though they'd never complain. The rest of us try to give him two nights a week off by taking Dad into our homes. When I call the nursing home back to accept, I learn that we have less than a week to deliver him, and that before they will take him, he needs a complete physical.

"What was that all about?"

He seems uncharacteristically focused, and when I meet his eyes, eerily rational. This has happened off and on, but not recently, at least not with me. There have been brief windows when he seemed lucid. In the parking lot at K-Mart where we had just bought him new rubber boots, he had a coherent moment. He popped in like an aside in a play and talked to me with clarity. He told me about his nursing home choice, some things about his will, and confirmed that he didn't want intrusive life support when the time came. When he had said his piece and believed I understood, he checked out again. When we got home, he got agitated and spent half an hour looking for the other two boots, the two he needed to make the set of four that would include his hind feet, like for a horse.

"Okay, do you remember talking about the nursing home at Ascension? You told me that when the time came, that's where you want to go. They called to say they're ready for you now and want you to come live there."

"What'd you tell them?"

"I said you were ready, and that you will come."

He's quiet but seems to be processing. I think I detect sadness in his eyes.

Later, we drive to the lookout at Cap Sante where we park the car and look across at the refineries, the anchored ships and the smaller boats moving in the bay. He soon gets bored and restless. I'm thankful for the seatbelt that he can't unbuckle without help. Before I take him back to Daniel's that evening, he tells me about the giant sheep he sees sliding down the neighbor's roof.

When his name is called in the waiting room, he doesn't recognize it. The doctor specializes in geriatric patients and the nurse is skilled at coaxing him through the weighing and measuring. She gets us settled in an examining room that is less like a clinic than most, with soft lighting and furniture that could go in a living room.

While the nurse is out of the room and before the doctor arrives, he starts telling me about how he has been mistreated by someone recently and how that person had hit him. He can't identify the person. I ask him if he's accusing Daniel and he says no. Daniel is rarely ever himself, as I am rarely me. He says he has bruises on his back. I gave him a shower this morning and for once he didn't accuse me of having homosexual motives. There are no bruises on his back.

The idea may have come from a television trailer he saw at my house, previewing a movie about a woman who is beaten by her husband who also attempts to have her killed. The preview showed the woman baring her shoulder and it's badly bruised. He tries to show me his shoulder in a way similar to the way the woman did on TV. He brings it up again when the doctor comes back. She has to report serious accusations and have them investigated. She'll decide whether she thinks this is real.

He's called the police on Daniel more than once. They did a thorough investigation the first time, but after they understood the situation, they only checked in with Daniel. Dad dropped the bruise story and the doctor seemed to pay it no notice. He has to have a rectal. Since the colon surgery he's had a problem with swollen testicles, so they have to be examined too. We undress him and as she is doing the examination, I can see on his face that alarms are going off in his head. I prepare myself for a real conspiracy hallucination about perverted sex. Instead, after he has his clothes back on and while the doctor is making notes, he surprises me with a question.

"Is there something you want to know about me?"

The light above the examining table he's standing beside is bright, almost harsh, compared to the rest of the room. He has that dark look, confrontational, defiant and challenging, the side of him I've dreaded all my life. He repeats.

"Is there something you want to know about me? Ask it and I'll tell you."

The doctor looks up, then goes back to writing. Physically, he's not imposing. He's a sick old man. He's not tall and has become almost slight, but the look still carries some of his old power and cuts into me. Is this the big moment, my last chance to breach the God wall and see the man? Whatever he says has to be put in the context of hallucinations of giant geese attacking a calf in a field, sheep or pigs sliding down the neighbor's roof, and giant slugs up his sleeve. I say,

"Is there something you need to tell us?"

"Ask me what it is you want to know!"

"We'd like to hear anything you want to say."

I get more of the dark, confrontational look. The doctor finishes writing and the moment passes.

Five

For the first five months of my life, my family lived in a normal house outside the city. Of course I don't remember any of that, but there are home movies and it looks like a comfortable, modest little bungalow with rose bushes in the yard and chickens and cats and a garden plot along the side. But my parents envisioned a better life for us, sold the house and, with a group of other Christians, convinced they were called to do the Lord's work, moved onto the leased grounds of a vacated tuberculosis sanitarium and renamed it Gethsemane after the garden in Jerusalem that Jesus and the disciples often visited to pray.

We lived on campus until I was six. I think I was happy during most of that time. I look happy in the home movies. My life was narrow, confined to the grounds with visits to my maternal grandmother, trips to my dad's family in Montana, and occasional camping trips. Most everyone we came in contact with was like us except my mother's mom, and she guarded her thoughts on religion.

We were poor, but there was good reason for it. We were serving God. My parents thought of themselves as missionaries even though we didn't go to Africa or South America or any place exotic. They seemed happy and to love each other. They were idealists trying to improve the world. I had a place to live, enough to eat, and other kids to play with. The sanitarium grounds were quite beautiful. It was not a bad place to be a kid. There were big lawns and fishponds. It felt safe and our parents let us have the run of the grounds.

By the time I was five there were six of us jammed into what had been a studio apartment for nurses when the sanitarium was in operation. The place had a tiny kitchen, a WC, which was small and truly closet-like with the old style flush-water tank mounted high on the wall above the bowl, the pull chain dangling. There was a bathtub in its own small room, and one big room that my parents modified into a combined living and sleeping area.

In addition to my parents' bed on the living room side of the plywood divider that separated it from the kids' sleeping space, there were a couch and a piano on opposite walls with a braided rag rug on the floor between them. The plywood was tacked between a set of bunk beds for two kids and the big adult bed. There was an old wardrobe at the end of the bunk beds that provided closet space and gave the area where we kids slept the feeling of being a separate room. There was a closet with no doors on it built into the wall opposite the bunk beds in the kids' space. My brother, who was then the youngest and would later change his name to Daniel, slept there. Lilly, who was the oldest, slept on a studio couch in the hallway. Katy and I had the bunk beds.

We were cramped, and when my mother got pregnant again, we burst the seams. My parents had bought two wooded acres less than a mile from the sanitarium grounds. "Easy walking distance," my mother would say. My father had worked evenings and Saturdays, carving out a home for us there. He usually worked alone, consulting books from the library and getting advice from friends to teach him what he didn't know about building a house. Sometimes the other men from Gethsemane would help, but it was my father's project.

When the baby came, another brother, there was clearly no place for him in the apartment, so we moved into the shell of the new house. It had been hastily roofed and the outer walls insulated. The roofing was nailed on as a communal effort, like a barn raising. There is a home movie of the men working on the roof and the picnic lunch. People seem to be having fun. We moved in while my mother was in the hospital, and camped out there.

The house was huge. When you're small, even a cramped house can seem big, and after the nurses' apartment, anything would have seemed spacious. But this house was truly large with three floors, six bedrooms and a family room. There were two-by-four studs where the walls were going to be, and knotholes in the subfloor that small toys and marbles fell through. You could spy through the holes on the people below. We used old bedspreads and blankets from the missionary store hanging on the bare studs to allow privacy where it was required. When it rained the basement flooded until eventually a cistern, a sump pump and a proper drain field were installed to keep it dry. We slept in sleeping bags in front of the fireplace the first winter. I remember liking it. It was an adventure.

When I was a kid, my dad was always working. In the circumstances he had created for himself, he tried to be the best dad he could. When time permitted, he was a patient teacher. He taught us how to work and occasionally we had fun with him. Considering how many of us there were and how busy he was, he did well, as long as he was dealing with printing, building something, or planting a garden, and as long as his truth wasn't challenged. And when we were children, we had little reason to challenge it.

During the week, he ran the print shop at Gethsemane. Above the print shop, the upper floors of the Monarch building housed part of the rest home. A brochure from that time, probably written by my mother, described it as having, "a congenial atmosphere for retirement at moderate cost. Landscaped grounds, trees, shrubs, flowers and pools set a keynote of beauty. Rooms are comfortable, and the Christian personnel show genuine love. Most appreciated is the rich fellowship of spirit in Christ, and for this reason many speak lovingly of their homes at Gethsemane Rest Home."

In a very real way, the print shop was an extension of our home. Before we moved off the grounds, I spent a lot of time in the building and playing in the beautifully kept formal gardens surrounding it. I knew the place intimately and felt comfortable there. I was given little jobs sweeping or collating, and sent on errands like trading the used type for the freshly poured lead *pigs* at the Powerhouse. Even as a preschooler, I was sometimes paid for my work and when I started first grade, I was paid to be there after school for an hour a day.

Each day I walked across the grounds from the elementary school to my job at the print shop. The early brochure gives the following description of the school: "Christian education is our goal. We not only try to teach academic subjects even better than they are taught in secular schools but, by relating these subjects to the Author and Creator of Life, try to point the pupil to the Way of highest fulfillment in human experience." My memories of it through the fourth grade are mostly good. I enjoyed learning and got good grades and I wasn't fat yet.

A covered walkway made of wood took me through the rest home, passing the old people's dining hall that smelled of coffee. Sometimes I talked to the residents on the main floor before I went through the heavy metal door into the cement stairwell that led down to the shop. Some of the old people were very nice and one guy gave me a cup full of arrowheads, which I still have. The basement was like a bunker with windows, and in the lowest floor of the rest home what little you could hear of the presses came through like white noise.

The print shop was an elaborate operation. At least a half-dozen people worked there. There were two big pressrooms, a dark room, a binding room, a typesetting area in one of the pressrooms, an art/layout room, and offices. The equipment included a Linotype, several presses of various sizes, a folding machine, a paper cutter, and a stapling machine. I was the boss's kid and

I think he was a good boss. I was proud of him. In addition to running errands and sweeping floors, I collated and stapled missionary letters and the monthly news bulletin that was sent out to supporters.

I worked there until the end of the summer before I entered the fourth grade. I was making ten cents an hour or fifty cents a week. The price of a candy bar is probably as good a way as any to measure inflation, and back then you could buy most candy bars for a nickel. The best ones were a dime, and though I bought other things like balsa gliders and toy cars, I had enough money for moderate amounts of pop and candy.

By the summer between third and fourth grade, we were well established in our unfinished house. My father was working on it room by room, making progress, though he didn't complete it until they moved out of it several years after I left home. We had chickens, rabbits, and a dog, a playhouse and a tree house. We built a shed out of a packing crate that a big printing press had been shipped in and got some goats. We did our chores and played in the woods. My mother wrote Christian children's books at home and had her own radio show on the Christian station, reading from them. She used our lives as her models, and in her books we had our struggles, but in the end we always "rejoiced in the Lord."

We walked to school at Gethsemane each weekday morning. If I was ready to leave when they were, I walked with my two · sisters, who were older. Occasionally, we were teased by the outsider kids who went to the public elementary school we passed on the way. When I was alone, they sometimes threw rocks. Even though we were still deeply entrenched in Gethsemane life, we had become commuters from the suburbs. We were also on the outside now, and our lives were beginning to change.

When my father started building our house, the site was quite isolated. Like nearly everywhere around Puget Sound, the old growth timber in our area had been logged, and the second growth was about forty years old. Most of the undeveloped land around us, and there was a lot of it then, was covered with this second growth. Our road wasn't paved. It wasn't even well graveled, and though the right-of-way went through to the next main arterial, it wasn't passable most of the time because of water.

It rained a lot, and in winter there was water everywhere. It flooded low spots, making ponds that were full of frogs and salamanders in spring. It flowed in creeks and ditches toward the small lakes that dotted the area or toward the Sound. Low spots in poorly maintained roadways like ours were often impassible mudholes in winter, and over a small rise near where it connected to a paved road, our road was blocked by a huge mudhole. Even in the summer, our road was so rutted and bumpy in the low spot that it was rarely used, so, in effect, we lived on a dead end.

There were some other houses scattered along our street. Most of them were twenty or thirty years old, no frills Depression-era houses. One of them was just a basement with the family living in it, waiting for the father to build the house on top. We weren't alone in the neighborhood or in our self-help dwelling circumstance. But the area was changing fast. Before we moved in, while my father was pouring concrete for the foundation, bulldozers had come and cleared land for more houses next to our plot, and shortly after we moved into our shell, we had neighbors who had moved into the new houses as they were finished.

The bulldozers kept coming and the trees kept falling; the swamps were drained and new houses were built on the cleared land. The roads were improved and shopping centers were built and sewers were installed until the woods were nearly gone, and with the trees went our Eden, our innocence and our happiness.

I think, now, that the trouble would have happened eventually even if he had said no that day. It just would have been different.

But my life changed dramatically the day one of the boys who had moved into a new house nearby asked me if I would take over his newspaper route during the week so he could play football.

The boy was older than me. I liked and looked up to him. The route was in the afternoon, and he was willing to make a fair split of the money. He only wanted to deliver on the weekends and would collect the payments from the customers. I rode my bicycle to the print shop and asked my father if I could, and he didn't say no, and after he talked it over with my mother, they said yes.

He let me go, and my memory of that day is my last clear, good memory of my father until years later, after I became an adult and the ceasefire was working and the fences were up, protecting the parts of our lives that wouldn't and could never mix.

It was called the paper shack, but it was really an attached garage, part of someone's house that was rented to *The Seattle Times* as a depot where we delivery boys could pick up our newspapers. The owners stayed out of sight when we were there. The papers were counted out in stacks for each route and labeled with the route number. One of the older boys was in charge of keeping order and signing off the stacks of papers. There wasn't much order but there was a code about the papers, and I always seemed to get the right number for the route. Whether that was true for everyone, or had something to do with the fact that the other boys were afraid of the boy I was working for, I don't know.

Fifteen or twenty boys met at this garage after school every day. I was the youngest, the kid. I had an advantage because of my neighbor's status, but I still had to prove myself. I was nine, at least three years younger than most of the other boys and, unlike them, went to school at Ascension Academy. They promptly took it upon themselves to corrupt me, and at first I tried to show my mettle by resisting, but the resistance didn't last long. I lost my struggle with my conscience. When I gave in the transformation was dramatic and I soon made a name for myself by becoming as foul-mouthed and rude as any of them. They were proud of me and protected me.

They gave me cigarettes, and though I made a valiant effort not to, eventually I started smoking. There was an alcove up in the rafters with a stack of nudie magazines. I didn't go up there because I was afraid of getting trapped and knew my protection was limited. But the magazines came down and were passed around, and I saw pictures of what the new words I was saying meant.

I had a great deal of freedom. Both my parents were busy, and in our family, work had a status just below piety. The work may have been valued more than the money, though the money was important too. As long as I was working I didn't have to explain much else about what I did with my time. I started buying some of my own clothes. I bought a new bicycle. I was conscientious, frugal and industrious, and I hardly ever saw my father. My body was also changing and I became very fat.

After several months, my neighbor wanted to quit the paper route, so I found another boy to share a route with. But, after a year or so, that deal also ended. I was too young to formally take a route on my own even though I had proven that I could do it. There were older boys waiting in line for afternoon routes and the paper company let one of them have the route that I had come to think of as mine.

The other newspaper company, *The Seattle Post Intelligencer,* delivered its papers at the beginning of the day and wasn't so choosy. They couldn't find enough boys who were willing to get up at four in the morning, seven days a week, so the district manager was delivering some of the routes himself in his car. When my parents agreed to it and were willing to sign a waiver, it didn't take much to get him to ignore the age requirement and give me a job. I became a small businessman and saw my father even less than before.

This time the paper shack was really a shack. It was a storage shed on the grounds of Gethsemane, where I had lived, where my parents worked and where I still went to school. The shed had no electricity and there was an old fire engine stored in the back, surrounded by boxes and crates of junk. Most of the year it was dark when we came to get our papers, and there were only three of us picking up there. When it rained we folded our papers and secured them with rubber bands so we could throw them and spend less time in the rain. Otherwise we rarely saw each other. On those rainy days we worked by flashlight and couldn't procrastinate long because we had to be done in time to go to school and customers complained about late papers. Complaints were penalized by the company and cost us money.

I learned to like the solitude of the early morning. Except for some menacing dogs and an occasional drunk, I owned the world. I liked my new bicycle and I liked the dark. No one could see how fat I had become and I could forget how much I hated myself for it. I could cut through yards. I could smoke cigarettes. In the summer I picked fruit from people's trees. I fed apples to horses and dreamed I was thin. To cover my shame, I found a black leather motorcycle jacket at the missionary store, started combing my hair like Elvis', and became a disappointment to my father.

In the winter, of course, the weather was sometimes awful and occasionally I would wake my mother and ask her to drive me around in the car. If the weather was bad enough, she would do it. It was nice to have the shelter and the heater and her company even if she did embarrass me most of the rest of the time. Not only did she preach to all my friends, but she was becoming a minor celebrity writing religious children's books and wasn't bashful about promoting them. Alone in the early morning rain and cold, she was good company.

I no longer knew how to talk to my father and he made me uncomfortable. Except for Sundays, I saw very little of him during this time.

It was a stormy morning or I wouldn't have asked, let alone actually gotten him up to drive me. It was windy, blackout dark. The rain was coming down in sheets and there was snow in it.

My mother was sick. She got up and looked outside, but she had been throwing up and felt awful. She knew she couldn't do it. When she saw what the weather was like, she made him get up, and from the start he was angry. While I was waiting for him to come out of their room, I heard him tell her that if I was old enough to take on the responsibility, I should be able to do the work by myself. She made him get up anyway.

I couldn't do anything fast enough for him. He would park and wait while I delivered to four or five houses along a street in the new subdivisions and he wanted me to run, which I tried to do. I was fat. I don't mean just a little chubby or round-faced with baby fat. I was under five feet tall and weighed 145 pounds and carried the kind of fat that made it hard to run. I was short of breath and no one knew better than I did how bad I looked. I was on a diet (my mother had taken me to a doctor) and was trying to lose weight, but it was coming off slowly. My father was mad at me for getting him up.

It was the word that tipped the scales. He said I *waddled*. I hated my body. Everything about it was bad. The nasty edge in my father's voice echoed what I was sure he would feel if he could see into my heart and know that it too was flawed with doubt about his God. The way he said it told me that he was as disgusted with me for being fat as I was with myself, and the fatness and my confusion about his religion, my secret guilt, caused me to hate myself.

Six

The clock says it's eight minutes before eleven. My mother would never allow me to oversleep and miss school. I look away and look back. The second hand is moving. When I got home at daybreak after delivering my newspapers in the dark, I put my bicycle in the garage and went back to bed.

I listen for the sound of someone moving about in the house and hear only the breeze rustling the bush outside the window. As I let my body wake up, I watch the light and the dark splotches of shadow moving on the wall next to me. A shriek on the other side of the glass makes my heart race. It's the banty rooster from the barn. It crows again. Peter had said he didn't know Jesus three times before the rooster crowed that morning. You can't hide from God.

I run to the kitchen. There's an empty cereal bowl, some silverware and the newspaper I brought home on the dining room table, but no note, nothing that tells me what I need to know. The teakettle on the stove is barely warm. "If therefore thou shalt not watch, I will come on thee as a thief, and thou shalt not know what hour I will come upon thee."

I yell for my mother and run upstairs, calling the names of my brothers and sisters. In my sister's room, the covers are arranged on the unmade bed in a way that she could have been sleeping under them and disappeared, been taken by the angels. In the bathroom there's water running in the toilet tank. I go in and jiggle the handle. There is no one here.

The dog is sleeping in the driveway. There are no cars on the road and no people. "I know thy works that thou art neither cold, nor hot. . . because thou art lukewarm, I will spew thee out of my mouth." None of the Catholics or Jews will be gone and only a few right-thinking Lutherans, maybe. If the Lord has come, you might not know immediately that anything has happened. If it's true, if He has come, maybe it will be on the radio. I'm afraid to know. I want to see Scout.

In the barn, the urine smell is strong, covering the normally pleasant smells of hay and horse sweat. I skirt the edge of the stall to avoid stepping in the manure with my bare feet. He's somewhere in the woods and I don't see him.

"Scout!" I yell.

A breaking branch snaps and I see movement in the trees. When he emerges from the salal, he nuzzles my hands and pockets for an apple or a carrot. I rub the side of his face and scratch behind his ears. He pushes my chest with his nose and I nearly fall backwards. I put my arm over his neck and feel his warmth.

Horses just live and die. It's simple for them, but I've missed my chance. It's too late. I've been deserted, left to suffer the wrath of God and to burn forever in the Lake of Fire. The earth will be ruled by Satan and the Antichrist for a thousand years. My born-again family has gone to Heaven, and I'll end up in Hell, after a life of misery.

My grandmother says being born once was enough. Sometimes after dinner at family devotions, we pray for her. I hope she's still here, and that I can live with her. I hope she'll let me keep the horse.

The hair on Scout's rump and hind leg is matted and caked with mud. He's nibbling at my pocket again and I feel bad for not bringing something for him. I lead him to a nearby stump and struggle onto his back. As he carries me through the stall doorway, I duck my head. He searches the manger for grain while I wonder what the pain of burning in the Lake of Fire will feel like.

When the cold starts getting to me, I slide down. The packed

manure, straw and wood shavings are unpleasant under my bare
feet. I wipe them on the grass outside and head for the faucet by
the back porch where there's a hose. Through the kitchen window I see a glint of reflected light moving.

My mother's glasses? She comes into focus, probably putting
away groceries. It's Saturday!

I don't know whether to run in and hug her or sit down and
cry. I remember my bare feet and know she'll want an explanation. I don't want to lie to her, so I go around the house and
rinse my feet at the other hose. I manage to get to my room, get
my boots on and head back to the barn to clean the stall without
talking to her.

I have to take a pill every day because the doctor says there's
something wrong with my thyroid gland and that's at least part
of the reason why I'm fat. I try to eat only what's on my diet and
only at mealtimes, but when I look in the mirror, I can't see much
difference. I'm still fat. I finish combing my hair and go out to the
dining room and sit at the table next to my father. He immediately says,

"I sat behind you in church yesterday and I was embarrassed
that you belonged to me. Your hair hangs over your shirt collar
and comes together in back like the tail end of a duck. You look
like a pool hall punk."

"If you cut it you'll give me a pig shave."

"What's wrong with a crew cut? You might look like a boy
again. If you don't want a crew cut, you can have a regular hair-
cut and part it on the side like any other wholesome Christian
boy. Now you look like a slob."

He's right. I feel like a slob but it's because I'm fat, not because
of my hair. I say,

"You don't care about me. You're not touching it."

"You're getting it cut tonight if I have to hold you down and shave your head, and don't think for one minute that I can't do it."

"You'll have to kill me first, you bastard!"

The blackness comes with the sharp impact, followed immediately by the tiny needlepoints of light swirling in front of my eyes. I feel the chair falling backwards. The floor between where I land and the front door is clear of obstructions. He is on the edge of his seat. My brothers and sisters are quiet, staring at me. My mother says,

"You didn't have to do that."

She sounds angry and about to cry. I stand up, watching my father, half expecting him to get up and hit me again.

"God damn you!"

As I say it, I run out the front door. Our street's been improved and the mudhole is gone. I run past where it had been, to the cross street, turn right at the corner and continue running a hundred yards or so, until I'm out of breath and my side aches. I cross the ditch and push my way through the salal and blackberry vines into the woods.

Under the tall evergreen trees the brush thins, and the ground is covered with soft needles. I sit down next to the trunk of a large fir tree and watch the road. Within a few minutes I see headlights approaching the stop sign at the end of our street and know by the sound that it's my parents' beat-up Plymouth. The car turns the other direction. I lean back against the tree and feel the left side of my face. It's sore but probably not bruised enough to turn color. I wish it were.

He never hits me with a closed fist. It's always a backhand and has only marked my face once. He was more wrong than me. It didn't matter what I had done, and he knew it.

Although it rained during the day, the ground under the trees where I'm sitting is dry and I'm sheltered from the wind. I have on a thin sweater. I know I'll get cold. I move so that the tree is

between me and the road and take the flattened package of Sa-
lems from the crotch of my pants. The package is bent and only
one of the four cigarettes isn't broken. I stole it full from a carton
in the kitchen cupboard at a friend's house. I don't like the men-
thol taste but my friend's mother drinks a lot and probably hasn't
missed them.

I light a cigarette and wish there was somewhere to go. I can
avoid my father most of the time except at dinner and on Sundays or when he drags me off to help work on the barn or build
fences at the property he bought. Getting us to spend time together is the reason they let me have the horse. He likes the horse
too. Sometimes when we're working around the barn, I almost
forget how much I hate him, but something always happens and
it starts again. I finish the cigarette and put it out against the tree.

I'm getting cold and wish I had been able to grab my coat.
If I wait long enough before I go home, there won't be a scene.
They'll have realized by now that I'm in the woods somewhere.
I always come back and I know they believe I will but aren't ab-
solutely sure, so my mother makes him drive around, looking.
Then he'll go off to a prayer meeting if there's one to go to, and
she'll be uneasy until I come home.

No one will talk about the fight. If my father is gone, I'll try to
make it to my room without being seen. She'll look in on me before she goes to bed. If I'm not there she'll look in the barn where
I'll be in the hay under the horse blanket, and she'll bring me my
sleeping bag and an alarm clock so I can get up early in the morning to deliver my papers.

We're on the tree-lined avenue—we called it the "Av"—that leads
from the main entrance past the nursing home, radio station, print
shop and high school buildings to the Ad Building. When I was
a baby, before moving to the nurses' quarters, we lived in the Ad
Building in an apartment above the offices and main dining hall.

It's spring, Missionary Conference time. Henry, the kid behind me on the horse, lives in the boys' dorm where missionaries' kids and kids sent by missionaries stay. He's my sister's friend and came from a village up in the Alaskan tundra. He likes riding and doesn't seem to mind that I'm a lot younger. As in other years, the army-green circus tent is pitched on the parking lot between here and the water towers. The door is open. Inside, sawdust covers the gravel, and a small late-afternoon audience is seated on rows of folding chairs.

If life is so hard, and our world is such a dangerous and threatening place, if heaven is so wonderful and a certainty for the saved, then maybe the missionaries who die in Africa or Ecuador are really just getting to bail out with a free ticket to a better place. If all those natives whom we're so proud of sending missionaries to can be sent to hell because they haven't heard the Word, maybe it's also true for the horse.

We could have just ridden by. As I guide Scout toward the open doorway I look back and get a quiet smile from Henry, like he gets what I'm thinking. He doesn't say anything or try to stop me. When we ride into the doorway, the man at the podium tries to ignore us. He continues speaking, but another man quickly rises from his seat. As he reaches for the bridle, I tell him that my horse needs to hear about God.

In a harsh whisper he spits the words, "Get out!"

Scout is tense. Balking at the noise and darkness, he takes no convincing to withdraw.

Henry and I have a laugh, a moment of feeling brave.

In addition to his dream of someday living here, my father wants to use this place to salvage me, to teach me the reality of work, the woods and his god.

We're alone, just the two of us. He's in the bottom of the hole wearing a tattered felt hat, filling the metal five-gallon buckets with mud and rocks. He's using a broken-handled shovel. His ragged bib overalls are tucked into his black rubber boots and covered with filth. There's a ladder on the ground next to me that I pulled up to get it out of his way after he climbed down. He made it from scrap lumber.

The last owners started this well. They had plans to turn the property into a kid camp or something and thought they needed more water than it would provide, so they tried to dig a deeper one next to the driveway. He says that hole went too deep. The seal was broken. It cut through the strata of hardpan and the water drained away in the gravel below.

Before we went to work on it, if someone hadn't told you this hole was here, you wouldn't have suspected. A thicket of blackberry vines completely covered it. The vines grew through and over the rotting fence posts lying side by side across it to keep kids from falling in. We couldn't dig it deeper until we cleaned out all the branches, rotten lumber, old wine bottles, jars and cans, the dead cat, and all the other rubbish that had fallen or been thrown in.

As he digs, water runs down the sides of the hole, oozing through the raw earth around him, trying to refill the well. When it gets too wet to work, he runs the noisy gas-powered diaphragm pump. The pump is expensive to rent and due back at the end of the day, so we have to finish. The hole has to be deep enough to have good water, even in late summer, but not so deep it breaks through the hardpan and becomes useless.

The cloudy sky and drizzle don't matter since we're wet anyway. The rope block-and-tackle centered over the hole hangs from a tripod made of three long pieces of rusty water pipe bound together with a piece of old chain. I pull a loaded bucket up, secure the block-and-tackle, unhook and dump the slop away from the hole, then lower the empty bucket back down to him. I tried going down the hole for a while, but I'm too slow. Up here I sometimes get a short break, but because he keeps an empty bucket down there to work on while I'm dumping, the work is steady enough to keep the wet from making me too cold.

This time the bucket is heavier and my hands are muddy. As I unhook, it gets away from me. The hole is deep. I have time to yell before it hits, but I picture him looking up at the sound of my voice and his glasses smashing as he takes the bucket full in the face. No sound comes out.

I've wanted to hurt him. I've daydreamed that he would be out of my life. If he doesn't move, the bucket will hit his back and break it, or break his neck, or at least an arm or leg. This is an awful dream coming true. Even with the excuse of cold, muddy hands, it's my fault the bucket is falling. There's no phone or even electricity in the cabin. I can't legally drive. I know I can't get him out of the hole by myself.

He doesn't see it coming, but moves just enough as the bucket hits. Its round side glances off his hip, and he doesn't make a sound, but does this epileptic dance down there in the muck to shake it off. After a few minutes when the pain seems to subside, he meets my eyes.

"Are you going to do that again?"

"No," I say.

He won't even let me put the ladder down. He goes back to work digging.

I keep pulling up and dumping buckets until the hole is as deep as he wants it.

Seven

The gun has always been there, in the brown leather shaving kit on the top shelf of the linen closet. I think he put it there when we moved into the house and we kids were small enough that we couldn't reach it. Then he forgot about it. It isn't even his. It belonged to my mother's father and has a dark history. We're fighting again, and I've escaped to the bathroom. If I'd stayed at the dinner table, I'd have said something to trigger the backhand.

I've looked at the gun before. This time I actually loaded it. I hold it in my hand, staring. The metal feels cool against my skin, the trigger against my finger. I carefully unlatch the door and step into the dark hallway. No one can see me. The kitchen light is off. I stand in the dark, holding the gun, looking across the kitchen over the counter that divides it from the dining room.

I watch him eat and even though I'm too far away to hear the smacking, I hear it in my head. I hated what I saw in the mirror and I hate what I see as I watch him at the table, eating. He's angry with me, and it makes his face ugly and his nose too big.

I feel the trigger against my finger and imagine raising my hand, aiming at his ear and squeezing. I imagine his body jerking as the bullet hits and the blood spraying all over the chair on the other side of him. The scene keeps playing, and I imagine the rest of the family's reaction. My mother's scream, and everyone crying and yelling, and I realize that I only hate him and myself, and the next move will be to point the gun at my own head, so I don't do anything. Pretty soon I go back in the bathroom and put the gun away. I can't even cry.

I can't look in the mirror, so I go back to my place at the table and try to eat. The food won't go down and the milk is thick and coats my mouth. I stare at my plate and try to let the room go out of focus and away. My father belches and it brings me back. I give him stomach problems and the doctor is afraid he's getting an ulcer. I can't sit here next to him any longer. I know if I open my mouth I'll say something that'll make him hit me. I want to hit him, but I can't do that any more than I could pull the trigger, so I get up and leave the table again.

Except for him, they all stop eating and watch as I walk across the room toward the entry hall where both the front door and the stairs up to my room are. Then my father turns in his chair and demands,

"Where do you think you're going?"

"Fuck off," I say back. I'm not sure he hears me.

"What did you say?"

"I said fuck off!"

I yell it this time and know I'd better get moving. I don't know why I go up the stairs. I guess I want *it* to happen, whatever *it* will be when I finally push him over the edge. I'm taller than he is and no longer fat, but he's my dad and way stronger. I'm scared of him.

By the time I reach the landing at the top, I hear him behind me and know I've made a mistake, so instead of going into my room I go into the bathroom where there's a window onto the roof. I bolt the door and climb on the toilet. The window's open and I'm trying to get my foot over the sill. If I get out in time, I'll hang from the gutter and drop to the ground. Maybe I can get away before he gets back down the stairs and outside. He pounds on the door.

"Open It!"

I'm trying to get out the window and get a foothold on the shingles. I hear wood splinter and see the door jam split. The

door flies open toward me. He has me, and pulls me back inside.
My foot catches on the sill and I twist my ankle. It hurts when I
put weight on it but he keeps me moving and throws me into the
hallway, then through the doorway into my bedroom.

I land on the floor and quickly get to my hands and knees.
He's standing in the doorway, and I expect him to come flying
at me with all that army stuff he keeps telling me he knows. The
dirty fighting stuff they taught him in boot camp so he could dis-
able a man and kill him if he had to.

"Don't you ever say that word again in this house!"

I'm dead anyway so I meet his eyes, and say, "I wish you
hadn't done it with her the night you made me, you bastard!"

I crouch like I learned in wrestling at school and brace myself for the army stuff. But it doesn't come. Something happens to
his eyes when he understands. I really don't want to be alive and
I hate him because I am.

"You mean that, don't you?"

I tell him I do, and instead of looking like he's going to kill me,
he looks like he's going to cry. He goes over and sits on the bed.

"You really hate me, don't you?" he says.

"Yes."

He's making me crazy again, only this is a new one and I don't
know what to do. The path to the door is clear. The door is open
and I could run down the stairs, but I can't make myself move.

"I'm sorry," he says. "I don't know quite how it got this far."

I stare at the floor.

"I don't want it to be this way," he says. "Will you help me
understand?"

I shrug.

"Will you at least try and talk to me and tell me what you're
thinking?"

"I hate you," I say. "I wish I didn't have to live here anymore."

"I'm responsible for you until you're an adult. It's the law, so I guess we're both stuck. I would like to try and make it better, but I'll need your help."

None of it seems real and I don't trust it. "I wish I'd never been born and I wish you were dead," I say.

"I hurt you that much?"

"Yes."

"Do you want to hurt me?"

"It wouldn't do any good," I say. "You'd still be my father."

"What would help?"

"Nothing," I say.

"Would you feel better if you hit me?"

It's hard to look at him, but I can tell he's serious. His eyes look like mine did in the bathroom mirror downstairs. None of it seems real and I hate him. The hate doesn't go away just because he didn't kill me and is blubbering on the bed. So I get up and hit him with the back of my hand the way he usually hits me. His face is like sandpaper and the impact hurts my hand. He winces and I can't look at him.

"Do you feel better now?" He's having trouble talking.

"No," I say.

"You still hate me?"

I hit him again, harder, and it hurts my hand worse. He takes it without moving and I make myself look at him. There are tears on his face, and I feel miserable, and I sit on the floor. I can't cry or think or feel anything except just awful.

And then I realize that for that instant we're equal and that he's just as miserable and helpless as I am, and that he doesn't have the answer either or he would use it and fix this. For a minute, that gives me a glimmer of hope. It's just a glimmer and it doesn't last long. It's like it isn't just my dad crying. It's as though God's crying too. I don't mean my dad's angry Lord, but the one I would believe in if I believed in a God, the one that would be big enough not to be angry all the time, big enough to forgive, and big enough to cry sometimes.

I also have this overwhelming foreboding that everything will turn to shit again any minute. And it does. Sort of. He looks up and says, "I'd like to ask the Lord for forgiveness and for his guidance in dealing with this thing between us. Will you kneel by the bed and pray with me?"

"I can't."

He looks at me for a moment before he says, "Will you at least keel with me while I pray?"

"No."

He kneels by the bed and prays aloud for a long time. I sit on the floor and try not to listen. When he's finished he says, "I'm going to leave you alone now. If you want to talk to me later, please do."

I don't say anything and he leaves. I listen to him go down the stairs and I don't know what it all means, but I know something is different. Of course I won't go and talk to him later. That's an invitation to give him my soul, the same as wanting me to kneel and pray with him was, and I can't do that. I don't trust what happened, and I have no idea what it means. He didn't hit me, but I feel worse than if he had.

The first impact of the back of my hand on his face wasn't enough, but the second time was like slapping a baby. He had given up, dropped his defenses and admitted he was helpless. He really didn't know what to do.

Eight

He's late getting the garden in. His back is to me and the noise of the rototiller covers my approach. He's wearing black rubber milking boots, baggy, faded, black Frisco jeans and a ragged denim jacket, not the close-fitting western style, but the baggy kind that old men wear. He still has all his hair, the gray is only over the ears, but the way he carries himself is slow, deliberate, like a tired, old man. I wonder what he wants to talk about.

When he's cleaned up and we're in the living room, he says,

"I'd have to be blind not to have recognized a change for the better in you since you've known her, but from what I've seen, I can't imagine that in the barely seventeen years you've been alive, you could have learned enough, become wise enough, to prepare yourself for what you're about to undertake. You're giving up choices you don't even know you have."

I say, "I know what I'm doing."

He doesn't know about how her boyfriend didn't stop when she said no, and that no one believed her, and about the unwed mothers' home, the baby that was adopted out.

He says, "You think you're in love and you probably are as much as you understand it. Love can be a very beautiful thing, but it can also be a terrible thing. If it's real, and if it's as strong as you seem to think, it'll keep until you're a little older."

I say, "You talk about choices. Before I met her, if I'd had the courage, I would have chosen not to be alive. If I hadn't met her, I might have found the courage. If all the awful stuff that you talk about actually does happen, it can't make me feel any worse than

I did then, and I'll have been happy for a while. At least now I'm glad I'm alive and I'm doing what I need to do, which makes me more free than I've ever been. Even if some of it is hard, I'll do the best I can. If I fail, at least I will have tried. It's not your problem and it won't ever be your problem."

"Haven't you ever gotten so fed up you wanted to explode like that?" I say.

"Have you?" Floyd sounds shocked. The story has upset him.

"I guess I can see how someone might if enough bad things happened to him," I say.

"He should have been hung by his balls," Floyd repeats and goes out the door towards the trucks. Floyd is easy to work with and I hope I'm not spoiling it. I start the tile machine and fall into a rhythm, feeding the mix and stripping the forms, still thinking about the guy in the news and the people he shot from the tower in Texas. He must have hated his own life so much that he didn't let himself think about what he was actually doing, about the innocent people who were dying.

He probably didn't think of them as innocent and maybe resented them, saw them as guilty because their lives didn't seem to be as awful as his. If life was hopeless for him, he thought it should be for everyone. He must have known he wasn't going to come down from there alive. You wouldn't do something like that with the idea of getting away with it unless you were truly crazy, and maybe he was, but you don't hang people by the balls for that. Even if you did it in a fit of rage, you would eventually have to face and live with what you'd done, and that in itself would punish you. Or, you would spend your life dodging responsibility, living false, and that would be its own kind of hell.

Was what he did that much different from killing people because they don't believe in your god, or because their politics are different, or dumping bombs on the Vietnamese because they're *gooks?* This Charles Whitman guy seems to think it's his world and he should be in control of it. So he decides that life is painful and pointless. *Give me liberty from the pain or give me death, and I don't care how many of you I take with me because your lives are pointless too. You are fools for not recognizing it, and if I take enough of you with me, either you will put me out of my misery or make me understand why I should continue to endure.*

This morning, with a box full of guns, he climbs a tower at the University of Texas to break out and throw it back at them. Sighting in on the first one, it wouldn't matter whom, just someone, one of *them*. He must have felt like God, knowing he'd already quit. What was still very dear to the people he was aiming at was meaningless to him and he had the power to take it from them. He probably just picked at random.

Even hearing the report of the rifle under his ear and watching as the first one fell wouldn't have made it real. He must have felt power. He did it over and over, watching them fall and watching the confusion as the rest of them tried to figure out what was happening, who would be next, and how to stop it, until someone finally got to him and killed him.

He must have wanted to die and was afraid of taking his own life. That would make him a coward. He was better off dead. He should have gone off somewhere and quietly checked out on his own. Sometimes people are a bunch of pigs, but becoming a bigger, uglier, more dangerous pig doesn't fix anything.

What if some guy like that shot Sandra?

The machine shrieks. The auger is jammed and the drive belts are slipping. The big electric motor strains to keep turning. The noise makes my whole body hurt. I push the stop button and look over my shoulder at the clock on the wall. It's a quarter to four. Until now, the afternoon has passed smoothly. The hopper in the tower above is full of freshly mixed concrete and I have to use it all before I can clean up and go home. It's already impossible to make the quota today and the old man in the office will say something to lay the blame on me. I won't get paid for staying late because, supposedly, it's my fault.

Sandra will have to wait outside the electronics plant where she solders circuit boards until I can pick her up.

I hope adjusting the blades will fix it and I won't have to change them. I pull the lever dropping the bottom table, releasing the cylindrical form. I open it. The mix drops to the floor, freeing the auger. The form is damaged, bulged by a piece of gravel bigger than the thickness of the tile wall. The gravel is graded and supposed to be small enough. I try to pick out oversize pebbles as I feed the machine. It's impossible to see them all.

I set the damaged form aside, pick the best spare and reset the auger blades. The first few tiles go smoothly. The auger drops, I feed mix as it comes back up. When the blades clear the top of the form, I lower and rotate the bottom table, placing a new form under the auger. While the auger is dropping, I quickly hit the full form with the rubber mallet. The auger is now at the bottom of the fresh form and I feed some mix. Quickly, I move the filled form onto the drying tray. I feed more mix to the auger, then strip the form on the drying tray, leaving the new tile next to the last one at the end of a neat row. I set the empty form back on the turntable in time to rotate it under the auger for the next cycle.

The tiles are each a foot long with a four-inch inside diameter, a short piece of concrete pipe. They're used, end-to-end, for making drain lines in septic systems. The effluent runs out through the cracks between them to be absorbed into the ground, distributed over the area of the drain field. They help dissipate the shit in the world and someone has to make them.

To operate the machine alone, you can't waste a move. It's like jogging, trying to keep up. The daily quota is based on the number of tiles the machine would produce, running continually for eight hours with a bare minimum of downtime. It requires two men, one feeding the machine and the other stripping the forms. One man can keep the machine running by doing both jobs while the other replaces a full drying tray or goes up in the tower to make a mix, but you can't run it alone all day, stopping to make the mix and move the trays, and be able to come anywhere near the quota. Even running with two men, it doesn't always go well.

I've made the quota alone once, or nearly alone. I ran the machine alone but Floyd made the mix and everything went smoothly. If the mix is too wet, the tiles stick to the forms and if it's too dry, they crumble when the form is stripped away. Everything has to be exactly right to keep the machine producing steadily.

I wouldn't mind working alone, even though it's harder, but the old man makes me feel like I'm not good enough. There isn't anyone to help now, anyway. No one stays long at the wages we make. I can't quit and the old man knows it. I make more per hour here than I could bagging groceries or at any other part-time job I could get, but the same work would pay more anywhere else, and I've been here long enough to be hard to replace for the price. He's given me a schedule with mornings off on school days to finish high school.

Sandra loves school and got me interested by sharing the books she likes. She made me read *The Scarlet Letter* right after we met. While she was still in school, she got me to do my own homework by studying when we were together. She was a good student before the unwed mothers' home. Becoming one of the top performers at her new school was her way of fighting back at the gossip and shaming that she had endured. Her old school was my high school before they kicked me out for getting married. The new girlfriend of her baby's father was in my classes. I'd been on juvenile court probation off and on since I was thirteen. I became the new development in their story about her, a new twist in the gossip.

She graduated from her new school with excellent grades and

is putting her dream of college on hold or giving it up, to be with me. I'm making good on my promise to graduate, and with her help, I'm starting to like school and do okay there.

I feed some mix. It's getting dry. I strip the form on the tray and the tile crumbles. I stop the machine, climb the ladder into the tower and add a little water. The old fart's face is at the office window. He watches whenever he hears the machine stop. The next tile sticks to the form and nearly cracks when I strip it. Too much water. I'll have to hit the forms extra hard. It goes smoothly for a while. My legs hurt.

The belts shriek. The auger jams again. I want to kill the machine. I want to hit it with something big. My body is vibrating. I push the stop button. The silence is deafening.

I free the auger. The form is sprung, bulged from another pebble. I throw it toward the pipe anvil for straightening forms and it hits the waiting pile of damaged forms. They clatter across the floor. It makes me feel a little better and I pick up the big wrench to adjust the blades. The door slams behind me and I turn to face him. He's angry. With the wrench still in my hand, I watch him come. He goes straight to the drying tray, looks at the tile, then at the forms on the floor. He feels the mix. He doesn't look at me until he's opening his mouth to start yelling. I watch him and something seems to register as our eyes meet. We stand silent for a moment.

"What's the problem?" His voice has its usual gruffness but it's more of a question than a challenge.

"There's a lot of big stuff in the gravel."

"Can you finish and clean up by quitting time?"

"I may be a little late," I say.

"Get busy then."

When I'm alone again, I loosen the bolts and adjust the auger blades. I'm sweating. My hands are shaking. I want to take a break, pull myself together, but I can't. I'll already be late. It's raining and she'll have to wait outside. I can't make personal calls on the office phone, and she might get in trouble if the call isn't a real emergency.

Nine

"Is he going to die?" I'm putting away the groceries I brought.

"No," she says, "but he's in the hospital. He's pretty badly hurt." She's in the living room and I can't see her.

"Well, what am I supposed to do about it?"

"He's your father!" She's in the kitchen doorway now. "Your mother wanted you to know."

"So now I know."

"He was riding that horse he's training, and it threw him. His foot got caught and he was dragged."

"How's the horse? If she isn't ridden again soon, this could ruin her. Did someone catch her and calm her down?"

"He's your father and he's hurt. He might have been killed. Both his arms are broken. One was smashed pretty badly. He's got broken ribs too. Your mother didn't tell me about the horse. She's pretty upset, and I think you should call her."

"What for? I'm not going to pray for him. How could he get thrown and dragged? He's always so goddamned cautious when it comes to animals."

"Well," she says, "It happened and he's in the hospital. I think we should go see him."

"What would I say to him?"

"It doesn't matter. He's hurt. Your mom said if we went today he's still too drugged and would probably be asleep, but we could go tomorrow afternoon."

"I have to study tomorrow."

"So do I," she says, "but this is more important."

He's lying on his back. One of his arms is in a cast and held above his torso by wires from a frame over the bed. The other arm is under the covers and also in a cast. Except for a few scratches on his face, his head appears to have escaped injury. He looks pale and needs a shave. She picked some flowers in our yard and is putting the vase on the counter under the television so he can see them when he wakes up.

"We shouldn't disturb him," I say.

She sits down in the chair near the bed. I lean against the windowsill and wait. Eventually he stirs and opens his eyes. He seems confused and disoriented at first, then surprised. After saying my name as though it's a question, he stops as if he doesn't know what to say either.

"How do you feel?" she asks.

"Sore. They've got me so hopped up on painkillers that I don't know whether I'm dreaming or awake." His voice is weak but he makes the effort to continue. "The Lord must have been watching over me. I feel pretty foolish. She was being so well-mannered, I guess I relaxed too much. I was wearing a hat. I reached up to scratch my head, and here I am. I guess they can fix me. I think it'll be a while before I want to get back on a horse."

"She needs to be ridden again soon," I say. My father's eyes have closed and he seems to be drifting off.

"She may be hard to catch," he says. "She got pretty spooked." His eyes stay closed and I watch to see if he'll wake up again, but he's asleep.

Through the alders, I see all five of them together, grazing in a small clearing. They're about as far from the barnyard as they can go and still be inside the fence. If I'm lucky, I can coax her with an apple, close enough to get a rope over her neck. Her name is Delilah, a joke name alluding to the lover who betrayed Sampson

that got shortened to Deli and stuck. I know that calling her won't
do any good.

When she raises her head and sees me, I'm still some distance
away. She snorts, but doesn't run off. I offer the apple, talking
to her, approaching slowly. She's tempted, but stops short and
stands, tentative, stretching her neck out, trying to get a bite. Then
she snorts and prances, wary of me, staying just out of reach. Her
fear and excitement are infectious. The sorrel mare, Deli's mother,
shadowed by the yearling colt, is now also on alert. The mare was
mistreated by her previous owners and is nervous and hard to
catch. She seems to have taught it to her young.

I let Deli bite into and take half the apple as I inch closer. My
father started working with her shortly after she was born, leading her and holding his arm over her neck until she was convinced that a restraint around her neck, whether a person's arm
or a rope, had the same power over her as a halter or a bridle. She
usually gives up and stands still. The others are milling behind
her. One of them crowds her and she comes forward toward me.
As she passes, I get my arm over her neck.

She bolts and I have to let go. The others follow and the herd
gallops off, snorting and bucking. I lose sight of them through
the trees. They stay on the tractor road, and it's easy to follow
their tracks, but instead of going toward the barnyard where I can
close the gate and maybe corner her, they've taken the fork that
leads farther into the woods.

My father and mother are back at the cabin. My mother offered
to help me, and now I wish I had let her. Though she tries not to
let it show, she's afraid of the horses, and I thought it would be
easier without her. Now I realize I probably won't be able to do it
alone and head back to get her.

Holding the broom from the cabin ready, she's wearing men's
rubber boots and an old skirt. The horses are running toward her.

She's in the open where she can't crowd them, so she's safe. Deli's in the lead and it looks as if, rather then turn in at the barnyard gate, they'll keep running right past my mother. My father is stationed opposite the gate, near a pile of fence posts and the tractor. He's only been out of the hospital a few days and can't move much, but he can yell.

At the perfect moment, my mother shouts and waves the broom. The horses veer sharply away from her and all five go into the barnyard. I run to close the gate. Deli and the other two Arabians pace, snorting, nervous in the confined space of the small corral. I go into the barn and throw some hay into the feeding box in the horse shelter. I leave the halter behind, take a bucket of grain into the corral and feed each horse a little by hand hoping to lure them toward the barn. Scout and the pony follow, but the others are too worked up and suspicious. I pour grain into the feed box and go out the back way to circle behind the three Arabians who are milling near the entrance, tempted by the hay and grain.

When I get close, the mare and colt go in, but Deli holds back. I move slowly, talking to her. She's cornered by the fence, and I think I have her. She stands like a compressed spring, facing me, her eyes wild. I inch close enough to touch her, but not in position to get my arm over her neck without moving fast, so I don't try.

Suddenly, she wheels and makes a lunge at the fence. She's too close to jump over and instead goes through. She doesn't get tangled, but the barbed wire rakes her legs and belly as the fence goes down. She runs off across the pasture, bleeding. The other horses come charging out of the barn and through the broken fence. The wire is close to the ground and they jump it without getting hurt.

I feel sick. I have to catch her and at least see how bad it is. My father, now next to me, looks at the fence, then looks after the horses across the field and says, "Might as well wait a while and let them calm down."

The sun is out and we eat lunch at the picnic table in the yard behind the cabin. My mother has made sandwiches and warmed some canned soup. She feeds my father and they don't talk. To avoid watching my father eat, I look instead across the field and see that the horses have come back from the woods. They're making their way toward the barn. We watch until they are through the open gate and eating the hay I scattered on the ground in the barnyard.

I can't think of any other way. I blocked the passage around the side of the barn before coming for lunch and repaired the fence, but I'm afraid she'll bolt again.

The other horses seem not to be paying much attention, but Deli is alert and only picking at the hay. My mother stations herself on one side of me with her broom, and my father is on the other. As we move in slowly, I see that the door to the milking stalls is open. It's a small walk-through door for people, like in a house, hardly big enough for a horse. I came out through it with the grain and should have shut it when I put out the hay. It's too late now. As we close in, the other two Arabians become alarmed.

Then the pony goes through the small door into the cow stalls. The other horses follow single file behind him.

Inside, the horses seem stunned, their shadowy shapes crowded into the cave-like darkness. The loft built above this part of the barn makes for a low ceiling, and there's little room for them to move about. There's enough hay on the floor to muffle hoof noise, and they're strangely quiet, watching me as I stand in the light of the doorway blocking the only way out. The air is thick with the smell of horse sweat and musty hay.

I don't move. I feel that at any moment, one of them will crowd another too close and they'll start kicking the walls out. My father appears behind me and says, "You should open the other door and let them out."

"No," I say, "I'm going in."

"You'll get hurt."

"It's the only way we'll get her."

I move an inch at a time, talking softly, soothingly. It seems to be taking hours. I come to Scout first and rub his neck, talking softly, gradually working around him. The pony is moving, worrying the others. The mare bites him when he gets too close. He squeals and darts toward the doorway where my father now blocks the way. I feel the rest of them tense up, ready to bolt and follow. I stay still, talking to them quietly, waiting.

They settle again and I ease toward Deli. Her muscles tight, quivering under the skin, she lets me stroke her neck. I keep talking and stroking until she calms, and I slip off my belt and slide it around her neck. I give her a piece of carrot from my pocket, then lead her past my father and out into the light.

The barbed wire cuts aren't as bad as I expected. There are several scratches that will probably heal on their own, but there are two deep gashes on the front of her left hind leg. My mother brings some peroxide from the cabin and I clean off the blood and dirt. I don't think they're bad enough to prevent me from riding her, but I'm afraid that if they aren't treated, they'll get infected. My father looks at the cuts briefly, over my shoulder, then goes inside to lie down.

She stands still while I saddle her. I'm careful not to move quickly and make sure she's expecting it before I make each move. When the saddle is secure, I lead her around the pasture until she seems calm enough. I put my foot in the stirrup. She sidesteps, but I'm able to swing up. I hold the reins short to prevent her from stretching her neck and getting her head down. She tries to rear and makes a lunge forward, throwing her head, straining against the bit, trying to get her head free so she can put it down between her forelegs and arch her back when she bucks.

She bucks two or three times, coming down hard and jarring, but as long as I can keep the reins short and her head up, the bucking is ineffective. She tries to run and buck, twisting her body to throw me. I grip the saddle with my knees and stay glued to it.

She rears again, high this time, twisting her head to the side and walking backwards on her hind legs. I feel her balance teetering. Afraid she'll go over backwards, I slack the reins and lean out over her neck. When she's down on all four legs, she realizes her head is free and bucks again, nearly pulling the reins from my hand. I keep my grip and am able to bring her head up short. She bucks a few more times, then stands still, trembling.

I pat her neck and let her stand for a moment while I catch my breath. My mother and father are watching from the yard. When I urge her ahead, she balks. I get her to walk around the pasture several times before I relax the reins. She has a comfortable trot and I guide her through a few loose figure eights before having her lope around the field.

When I dismount she's drenched with sweat and there's foam under the saddle pad. It's more from nerves and the trauma of the experience than the workout, and I walk, leading her around the field several times before tying her to the rail fence in front of the cabin and removing the saddle.

My mother comes out. "I'm glad that's over," she says. "I made him take a pain pill and lay down."

"I want to go to town and talk to the vet about those cuts," I say. "Will you watch her while I'm gone?"

"I can't stop her if she tries to get away."

"I don't think she will now. I won't be gone long."

The vet is gone but his assistant telephones him, then gives me some penicillin, a big syringe and some antibiotic salve. She says the penicillin will help prevent infection while the wounds close up and heal. It isn't the ideal solution, but Deli's too hard to catch to ask the neighbor who's feeding the animals now to treat her every day with the salve. Giving her the shot is better than doing nothing.

My mother is sitting in the rocking chair on the porch, in front of the horse, reading. When I get out of the car she says, "Your father is asleep. This has been a big day for him."

"I'm going to need your help with this," I say.

"I've never seen him so upset," she continues. "When the horse was bucking, if he could have used his arms, I think he would have shot her from under you."

"You mean he would have shot me off her or shot us both."

"He loves you."

"Bullshit."

"Don't talk like that. He kept saying that no horse is worth this much grief. He loves you and he was afraid you would get hurt like him, or worse."

"I have to stick the horse with this needle and I need you to help me," I say.

"Can't you just put the salve on her?"

"It's my fault she got cut up and I'm not going to turn her loose until I've done everything I can to make sure she heals right. The woman told me how to do it."

"It wasn't your fault. He said you couldn't have known she was going to do that."

" Will you hold her for me?" I say.

"Can I leave the rope tied to the fence?"

"Yes. I just want you to distract her. Talk to her. Scratch her under the chin."

I rub alcohol on Deli's neck where the woman showed me on the horse at the vet's office. I fill the syringe and bleed the air, then start tapping the prepared spot with my left hand while holding the syringe in my right. I tap lightly at first, then harder, then jab the needle in. She flinches. Her body tenses. My mother holds Deli's head and keeps talking to her the way she would to a baby.

I push the plunger, slowly forcing the drug into the muscle. When it bottoms, I pull the needle out and wipe the sweat from my forehead. "That wasn't so bad, was it?" I say.

My mother says, "Your father will be proud."

"Yeah, I'll bet."

After I give the wounds another look, dab some more peroxide on and slather on a good coat of salve, I lead the horse around
the field again. When I'm passing the house on my way back toward the barn to let her go, my father comes out to meet me, and
for the first time today, I actually look at him. Both his arm casts
are taped close to his body. His fingers are free and he can move
them, but without the use of his arms he can't feed himself or
even wipe his own butt.

"I'm afraid I wasn't much help," he says. "Thank you."

Ten

She's struggling not to pass out. I half-carry, half-drag her from the doctor's office. No one offers to help. Besides feeling desperate and scared, I'm angry now. I brought her here because she had severe abdominal cramps and was throwing up and fainting. She's pregnant, in spite of the fact she's been conscientious about using birth control. We have no medical insurance and came to the clinic because it's near the school and someone said its fees were low. There's no hiding that she has given birth before and the doctor clearly doesn't approve of us. He treats her like she is a whining child, says the symptoms are part of a normal pregnancy, and tells her to go home, take an aspirin and lie down.

We're going to community college together, barely getting by, but she had hope again and our life together felt good. We've known about the pregnancy for a month maybe. It's tearing her apart because she was finally able to quit her job, has been taking classes and enjoying her life as a student again. We both have part-time jobs and, along with student loans, get a small poverty grant from the financial aid office.

I see a phone booth, get her settled in the car and run across the street. The phone book is a mess but I'm able to find the number and call a gynecologist she saw when we had insurance from where she worked. I describe her symptoms to the nurse. They seem to mean something to her and she brings the doctor to the phone. He says to bring her in immediately.

The nurse is waiting with a wheelchair and quizzes us as we go inside. Sandra is getting weaker and can barely whisper. She can no longer sit up. Her hair is damp with perspiration and her eye make-up is smeared. The doctor meets us in the hallway. In the examining room, he feels her abdomen and asks me more questions. I tell him about the other doctor and what he said. He asks me to wait in the hall for a few minutes.

When he comes out, he says, "This may be serious. She has the symptoms of a tubal pregnancy and may be bleeding internally. Take her to the emergency entrance at the hospital. If you leave right now, you'll get there faster than we could in an ambulance. I'll meet you there. They'll be expecting you."

On the way, she wakes up.

"Where are we going?'

"To the hospital. The doctor thinks you have a tubal pregnancy."

"You can die from a tubal pregnancy," she says.

"You're not going to die."

We're quiet the rest of the way. I have to wait outside the room while they prep her for surgery. When I'm allowed back in, they've combed her hair and washed her face, but she looks worse. I wonder if this is the last time I'll see her. Her doctor comes in. His presence makes me feel more secure. She whispers that she can't breathe well and that she wants to sleep. The doctor is silent, then asks me to step into the hall with him.

"The operating room is being used right now. They'll finish in a few minutes and we'll be able to go in. It will take at least two hours. Be in the lobby by seven. I'll meet you there."

He avoids meeting my eyes and hurries off. I walk beside the gurney as they wheel her to a set of double doors where I'm not allowed to follow.

I can't help by staying and don't want to wait alone, wondering, for two hours, so I drive to my parents' house. I knock and, without waiting, enter. The family is seated at the table. My mother is bringing food from the kitchen and invites me to join. I find an empty chair.

"Where's Sandra?" my father asks.

"In the hospital," I say and tell my story.

"It's good you didn't take the first doctor's advice," my mother says.

"Why don't we pray for her," my father says.

My father bows his head. They stop eating. I watch as he prays. I feel numb and very alone.

"Our father, we know that you are the author and finisher of events here on earth and that you have a reason for everything. We ask that you be with Sandra now through this difficult time and that you guide the surgeon's hands and, if it's your will, bring her and the baby safely through it. We ask also that you be with Bill tonight in this time of trial, and that he'll recognize his need to be close to you. We thank you for your grace and blessing. Amen."

I wish I had stayed at the hospital. If it makes my father feel better, I don't care if he prays, but I don't like acknowledgement of my need, as my father put it, being tied to her safety. Whenever there's a crisis they find a way to word their prayers so they became a form of coercion. I resent the implication that now, because her life is in danger, I'll be afraid enough to see the light, to bargain with God, to repent and become born-again.

"I'm going back to the hospital," I say.

I'm glad when they don't insist on coming with me.

Back in the lobby, I worry that the doctor has been there, not found me and gone home. I'm afraid to ask the receptionist, afraid to know. I leaf through a magazine but can't read anything. I make myself go to the desk. The woman says she hasn't seen the doctor.

"I'll page him," she says. "If he's still in the operating room, he won't hear it, but if he's anywhere else in the hospital, he'll call me."

We wait. The doctor doesn't call. If she died, he wouldn't still be in the operating room. Then I feel someone standing above me. He's still in his surgical suit and looks tired. There's no hint on his face of what happened. He pulls up a chair and sits down.

"She's going to be fine," he says. "You can see her when they take her back to her room in about an hour." He goes on to explain that she had been bleeding internally and they gave her three pints of blood. She nearly died and the fetus had to be aborted, but there was no permanent damage to Sandra. She had an abdominal pregnancy, which the doctor says is rare. When he's gone, I call my parents. My father answers.

"We were praying for her," he says, then asks if I want to come spend the night.

"I think I'd rather go home."

Even asleep she looks better. The color has returned to her face. There's an intravenous bottle hanging above the bed with a tube running into her arm. She wakes up groggy.

"You're going to be okay," I say, "and there's no baby now."

The loss of a baby is supposed to make you sad, but for us it's a huge relief. The pregnancy had returned Sandra to the nightmare of the unwed mothers' home and condemnation from everyone in her life. It was shattering the dream of reclaiming her life. And I'm not ready to be a father.

She soon falls back to sleep. I dread going home. It makes me feel good to watch her breathe.

It seems to take forever to clear the driveway of the other cars so we can get out. When people heard why they had to move their cars, the party broke up and Sandra decided to come too. I have to concentrate in order to drive. Earlier I smoked part of a joint and it makes the lights too bright and distracting and everything seems slowed down. As I turn the car onto the freeway on-ramp, Sandra breaks the silence

"He'll probably be all right," she says. "At the hospital, they'll know what to do."

"He's got to be," Ben says. "I can't believe we're doing this, that this is actually happening."

Ben's sister had found their brother on the floor at their house, unconscious, a hypodermic needle still in his arm.

I park near the hospital's emergency entrance. I expected it to be lit up and active, but it's dark and looks deserted. There's a parked ambulance near the doorway. Ben and his girlfriend run into the building. The reception desk is well-lit but unattended. There are doorways along the hall but the doors are closed. Eventually one opens and they come out. When I see Ben's face, I know.

"He's dead!" Ben says it.

"They didn't even bring him inside," Ben's girlfriend says. "He's still out there in the cold."

While we wait for Ben to sign some papers, I notice that Sandra is gone. I find her standing at the back of the ambulance, looking in at the body. His eyes are closed and he almost looks asleep, but there's something wrong and unnatural with his face and the way his body is positioned. She's crying and I take her hand.

"They didn't even cover him," she says. "I've never seen anyone dead. The only thing that died that mattered to me before was my dog when I was small. He got hit by a car, and we buried him in the garden. For a long time afterward, I couldn't stop crying or get the picture out of my mind of him lying there in that hole while my father put dirt over him."

"I have to. I can't explain it to you, but I know I have to," she says.

She looks down at her plate. There's no anger in her voice. She's almost apologetic.

"You're serious this time, aren't you?" I say.

"Yes." She looks up and I know she means it.

"What did I do? When you're unhappy, I try. You're in school now. I help with the cooking and the housework."

"I know. That's not it."

"Well, what then?"

"I don't know. I can't explain it. I just need to be alone, to think, to figure out who I am. I don't know anything anymore. I don't know what I feel or who I am. I don't know what love is anymore or if it even exists. I can't love you now the way you want me to, and if I can't do that, it isn't fair for me to stay here. I don't love anyone, not even myself. I like you and I don't want to go away and never see you again, but I don't want to be married to anyone either."

"What happened?"

"I don't know. I have to do this," she says. She's almost crying. "Please don't make it harder."

I take the vacuum cleaner and hose from the back seat of the car and set it on the sidewalk. I pick up the lamp, some file folders and a box with a clock radio and some letters and knickknacks in it. It's all I can do to hold the assortment in both hands. I push the back of the front seat upright again and, with my foot, try to shut the door. The door hits the vacuum cleaner and sends it skating across the sidewalk and off the curb by the rear tire.

I kick the door closed and leave the vacuum canister where it is. I carry the other things up the steps to her apartment door and knock. I hear footsteps inside. She slides the chain open, then unlocks the door. She's expecting me.

She smiles and says, "Hi."

I don't answer right away. I hate it when she tries to pretend that everything is fine and we're just old friends having a nice visit. I walk past and put my load on the floor near the coat closet. A stack of my books waits by the telephone. "I'll be right back," I say.

When I return with the vacuum, she's sitting on the couch, watching television. She smiles and says,

"The news is on. Why don't you stay and watch it?"

They're showing scenes from Vietnam with machine guns firing and helicopters flying low over a village. I want to leave, but I pull the chair we reupholstered out from the wall to get a better view of the screen and sit down.

"Have you eaten yet?" she asks.

"Yes."

"What did you have?"

"Leftover pizza."

A drop of sweat runs from my armpit down my side and feels like a bug crawling. I take off my coat. "It's hot in here," I say.

She gets up and turns the dial on the thermostat. "The switch is broken and it doesn't turn itself off. The manager said he would fix it, but he hasn't yet."

I watch her walk back to the couch and check my impulse to offer to replace it for her. She looks even better now than she had before. Her hair is different and she looks healthier. I want to sit next to her and to hold her and have her laugh and love me back. I want the chair to still be in our living room and I want to still belong in it.

"How's your mother?" she asks. "I miss talking to her."

"Fine," I say. I know I can't sit here much longer talking like this, so I try to let her know with a look what she's doing to me.

"What's wrong?" she says. She sounds defensive.

I hesitate, then say, "I have to go." I cough to clear the tightness in my throat. "I'm seeing a lawyer tomorrow. He wants a list of what we own together and who gets what."

"Unless you want something that's here, I'm happy with it the way it is," she says.

"I told him I would pay off the loans we got together for school and for the hospital bills with the money I get from selling the house. If I sold it right now there would be just enough. You'll get a copy of the final papers and a notice when the court date is set. If it looks all right to you, don't come to court. They'll just stamp it and file it and I'll be out of your life."

I try to remember anything else she might have of mine that would bring me back. She has my wool shirt. It's navy blue and heavy and she likes to wear it like a jacket but it's mine. I bought it before I met her. I go to the coat closet. As I open the door she's beside me.

"What are you looking for? Let me find it."

"My wool shirt. What are you trying to hide? I don't care if Craig keeps his things here or if you keep a fucking army of men in your closet. Keep the damn shirt." I turn towards the door. She's rustling around in the closet.

"Wait," she calls. "Here it is."

I take it from her. My hand is on the doorknob when she says, "You've always thought I was bad."

"You think you're bad and try to prove it to me," I say.

She's huddled on one end of the couch with her legs folded under her, arms crossed over her breasts. Her eyes are wet. I go to her. "Please look at me," I say.

She hesitates, then meets my eyes. I see fear and pain. "We always hurt each other," she says.

"It can't get much worse than this," I say, "But we can't seem to stay away from each other, can we?"

She gets up and turns off the television. I watch her move. I light a cigarette and pull the dry acrid smoke into my lungs. It seems to help appease a hunger. I slowly exhale the smoke, watching it as it flows across the room toward the kitchen.

"Can I have one?" she says.

I light another and hand it to her. I don't know what to say. We can't undo what's been done and it isn't as simple as just forgiveness. It's unbearably painful when we play it her way and talk small talk, so I fight it. Even though she's admitting that she hurts too, it doesn't change anything, and we don't have much to say.

We smoke in silence. A bus goes by and hisses to a stop at the intersection. There's the thin wail of a siren off somewhere in the darkness. I watch her smoke.

"What do we do now?" I say. "This is too hard. It would be better for me if we don't see each other at all unless we're willing to start over."

"I like you and I like to see you, but I don't want to be married to anyone."

The feeling of being an intruder in her life is gone for the moment and I don't want to go, but we're at an impasse and I know I shouldn't stay any longer.

"I don't mean to hurt you," she says.

"I know," I say. "And I don't mean to hurt you."

I let myself out the door.

Eleven

I would have dropped out of the University of Washington my junior year, had the break-up not coincided with Vietnam War-related turmoil on campus. I was depressed, unable to concentrate on my schoolwork, barely able to function. For me, the campus unrest was the background noise, the soundtrack and external reflection of my despondency. If I dropped out of school, I would be drafted. Uncle Sam wanted to give me a gun and send me to Vietnam. The world felt malevolent. My future seemed like a nightmare.

That was the year of Kent State. The UW administration building had been bombed in June of 1969. Large rallies and demonstrations were common, often accompanied by cops in riot gear. My world had collapsed and it felt like the world around me was collapsing too.

I first became aware of Vietnam when I was fourteen on one of those rare, actually warm days in May. I was part of a group of kids gathered on the new asphalt parking lot at the base of the sandy bluff at Richmond Beach. It would be two years before I'd be old enough to drive, but the loud pipes drew my attention to my dream car, a Fifty-six Chevy two-door hardtop, as it came down the hill. The car parked beside us. It was clean, beautiful, with baby moons and chrome exhaust. Everyone seemed to know the kid. He was shirtless, buff, and with a can of Rainer beer in his hand, he slammed the door and announced,

"I can't wait to get to Vietnam and kill some *gooks!*"

I had no idea what he was talking about.

The bridge over the railroad tracks, part of the transition from industrial site to park, was unfinished, useless, ending in a six-foot drop to the sand. A trail led through the blackberry jungle and crossed the tracks. On the shore, charred keels were visible at low tide, bedded in the muck beside a row of piling stubs. Newer ships made of steel were replacing wooden ones and the burning had ended only a few years earlier, but the ship remains seemed ancient. On the trail, I heard that the Chevy driver was in some new trouble and wasn't going to graduate. He had just enlisted in the army.

It took me by surprise that we were in a war and someone close to my age would be involved in it. I had been too young and had paid no attention to the Korean War. Besides the Cold War and its ever-present nuclear threat, World War II was the war I had given thought to, but the crumbling sandbag and cement piers that I had played on as a kid seemed as antiquated as the ship spines. The piers supported a ring of protective anti-aircraft firepower around the navy base near my grandmother's house. They were built only a few years before I was born for protection from a feared Japanese invasion during World War II, but they were relics of the remote past.

Before I finished high school, Vietnam had gained considerable significance in my life, and on my eighteenth birthday, a month before graduation, I was called to the vice-principal's office and required to register for the draft. I was finishing high school to fulfill a promise to my mother, the judge at the emancipation hearing, and the girl I had left home to marry shortly after my seventeenth birthday.

When I flunked my draft physical my twenty-second birthday was only weeks away, and the failure of my four-year marriage was official. We were two broken kids, struggling to find a place in the world. Our individual baggage complicated each other's attempts to heal. We had been friends, but the bonds of friendship were overshadowed by the complexity of marriage while so young and so damaged. I like to believe we helped each other, and in the end forgave each other for not being big enough. She taught me to value human connection, and our break-up didn't destroy that. I wanted the sense of belonging and trust I had glimpsed.

I met my wife, Allie, at a University District cabaret in Seattle while celebrating my flunked draft physical. She and I are in Vietnam as I write this, celebrating our forty-fifth wedding anniversary. We're spending money saved over several years, set aside for a trip to mark our fortieth, postponed because of problems with my health. As a vacation destination, Vietnam at first seemed far-fetched.

We had heard the country is beautiful, but in my mind, it was still a scary place, like Red China and Russia. The people in these countries had been our enemies. I have nuclear-holocaust, duck-and-cover-drill memories from elementary school through high school. My college friend, Ben, is also on this trip. He owned a view house above Lake Washington built during the Cold War, with a bomb shelter under the driveway. But the world has changed, and Southeast Asia seems relatively stable. Affordability and favorable reports from friends drew us to Vietnam.

To show how well-hidden the tunnel entrances at Củ Chi were, a kid with a clear-eyed smile in a Vietnamese army uniform emerges from the ground holding the leaf-covered tunnel plug above his head. He seems unaffected by our being Americans and that the spent bombs on display here were dropped by our planes. The passion of one generation is not easily passed to the next. I was close to his age when the war touched me most. It had likely ended by the time his parents were born.

Củ Chi is a park now, a museum of history, a monument to national pride. Open sheds display bomb casings as historical relics. A Huey helicopter carcass greeted us in the parking lot. The

B-52s that dropped the bombs are long gone, and you have to look closely beneath the trees and brush that reclaimed the land to see the craters left by carpet-bombing, even though they're everywhere. The Tết Offensive of January 1968 was orchestrated here, and there's a large crater next to the command bunker. Roots from a stand of bamboo protected the underground shelter from caving in.

To the kid showing us around, the war must have the same disconnect and lack of immediacy as relics of World War II had for me when I was his age. *But the Tết Offensive was real to me.* Even though it was on the other side of the world, I followed news of it closely as it was happening. My government wanted me involved in it. A booby trap, proudly displayed here, designed for use against American soldiers makes me imagine the life I might have lived, maimed by it or maimed by the psychic booby trap of the war itself. To put off being drafted, I had enrolled at a community college. In 1968 during the Tết Offensive, instead of working construction, I was a freshman.

I stoop and follow an elderly (my age) American doctor through an enlarged (for Western tourists) Viet Cong tunnel. With the help of occasional electric lights and the ibuprophen pills I took on the bus for the stiffness in my back, I crawl through the tight passages and stand in the bunkers, trying to imagine actual people braving scorpions and snakes, eating, cooking, performing surgery, and planning strategy in these claustrophobic holes. Air vents, cooking smoke vents and spy holes are disguised by termite mounds and brush. The smoke vents were ingenious, directing the smoke through three chambers so it came out of the ground clear.

The Vietnamese people are trying to heal. Vietnam has been an independent nation since 1975 and time has diffused the passion, the hatred of the French, then the American occupation that inspired what happened in these tunnels. The posed dummies on

display in the field hospital, sandal factory and command-post
bunkers fail to deliver the intensity of the history they represent.
Though the mannequin scenes at Củ Chi lack immediacy and
have a department-store exhibition feel, I find that my memories
related to and inspired by the tunnel occupants' passion aren't far
below the surface.

*The room I'm in is like an ordinary classroom on campus. There's a
blackboard up front, and the rows of desks have a comforting familiarity. The first part of the test was similar to the Washington Precollege
Entrance Exam, only with more emphasis on determining mechanical
ability. At the big desk where, at the university, the professor would sit,
the man is wearing a uniform, and the questions in this section of the
test are different from school exam questions.*

*It's the middle of April, and I'm here for the pre-induction physical
and testing. I drew a low number in the draft lottery and they're wasting
no time. My student deferment has expired. My status is now 1-A and
if I pass the physical, I'll be in uniform within days of June graduation.
I'm surprised at how calm I feel. It's too late to worry. In spite of much
alcohol and little sleep over the past few days, my head is unexpectedly
clear. I feel lucid and believe I've done well on the exam.*

*"HAVE YOU EVER ATTEMPTED SUICIDE?" There's a box for
YES and a box for NO.*

Lying on her side, retreated deep into herself, she hugs her knees.
She doesn't respond to my pleas. I leave the room. I wish there
was something to drink, but her father drinks and she doesn't
want it here. I feel helpless and guilty. The only thing I want from
life is to make her pain, our pain, go away, to be able to connect
with her, but as my father always does to me, I've pushed her into
herself again, and I don't know how to draw her back.

Her father couldn't have crossed the border with it, so he left
the gun here on his way to Canada. Taking the pistol with its

loaded magazine from under the folded towel in the drawer, I sit on the couch. I push the magazine into place, release the safety and look down the black hole of the barrel.

If I can't connect with her, I can't touch anyone or anything, so it won't matter, not really. I wonder what it will feel like, if the stories about your life passing in front of you are true. I don't think it will hurt much, or at least not for long. If I squeeze the trigger, there will be noise and blood.

If I do it now, she'll have to face the mess. If it were me finding her afterwards, I'd have to do it. She must feel as awful and helpless as I do. She might also want as badly to find a way through it. If I quit trying, it'll be my fault we failed.

I put the safety back on and lay the gun on the couch next to me.

The bedroom door clicks. The hinges squeak and she says, "Are you going to shoot me?"

She had actually thrown herself down the stairs at the unwed mothers' home. I didn't pull the trigger. Do I check NO?

The tide is coming in. Stubs of charred piling, remnants of an old pier, extend into the bay. Frost on the bleached logs reflects silver. The full moon backlights skeletal branches of the maples near the tracks and a thin, wispy cloud streaks the sky. A train around the point sounds its whistle. As it passes, the headlamp sweeps the tracks, cutting the darkness, destroying the good memory of being here with her. She's gone and I want to erase myself.

Shedding my clothes, I sprint toward the moon's reflection on the motionless water. I lunge through the liquid ice until my feet no longer touch sand. Cold sucks my breath. I swim clumsily away from shore. I want the cold to draw the fire out, numb me, take me.

My body disagrees. Before I'm swallowed I find myself struggling toward the beach. Sand finally beneath my feet, teeth chattering violently, I step on a broken clamshell and fall, then struggle out of the water. Gathering my clothes, I dry myself with the shirt. My fingers can't do the zippers but, at this moment, body pain has displaced anguish.

"Have you ever attempted suicide?" They want to know if I have the will to fight for my life, if I'll make a good soldier. The army dream often plays itself in my mind. In it, I'm in Vietnam.

Helicopters hover like giant hornets creating hot wind and brain-scrambling noise. We're going into an enemy village, mopping up, looking for survivors. The village has been strafed and bombed. There are bodies everywhere, women and children. I'm looking over the remains of a hut and find a boy, a child, not more than ten years old, hiding among some large baskets under a straw mat. He points a gun at me. I have to shoot or be shot.

I write in the answer-sheet margin, "If I had made a sincere attempt I guess I would be dead, and I'm not, but I loaded a gun once and looked down the barrel for a long time."

When I'm done and all the forms have been collected, there's a short break, then a sergeant comes in and briefs us on the procedure for the physical. After that, an officer reads some names, including mine. We're supposed to stay behind.

The desk in the small office is crowded with neatly arranged papers and manuals. The officer behind the desk introduces himself and looks at the file folder in front of him. He's in his mid-thirties. Leaning back in his chair, his informal, almost warm manner surprises me.

"Before we go to the expense, taking a lot of our time and yours, testing and psychoanalyzing you, do you have any physical problem that you think might disqualify you from military service?"

"I have a back problem," I say.

"Do you have it documented?"

"I have a letter from my doctor. I sent a copy to the draft board, and

I have one here with me."

"Let me see it."

He reads the letter. I started seeing the doctor who wrote it when I was nine and fat. He listens to me, so I still go to him. They found an abnormality in my lower vertebrae when I injured my back unloading a cement mixer from a truck. I was working for a brick mason as a hod carrier. The officer takes some forms from a drawer and writes on them. When he's finished, he hands the folder to me. "Take this down the hall through the big door into where the others are. Inside, give the folder to the doctor in the second office on the left. When he's through with you, come back here."

The door to the second office on the left is closed but has a chicken wire glass window and I see a man in officer's uniform at the desk inside. Behind me, the other guys are getting undressed and lining up behind a yellow line painted on the cement floor. I go into the office. The man continues writing and doesn't look up. Finally, he says,

"What is it?"

I hand him the folder.

"Who sent you?" His face is expressionless and his manner stern.

"His office is across from the testing room. I think his name is on the forms."

He opens the folder, glances over the forms, then writes on them, stamps them, closes the folder and hands it back to me. He goes back to what he was writing when I interrupted.

I ask, "Is that all?"

"That's it," he says without looking up.

I take the folder back to the first office and wait while that officer finishes talking to someone else. When I'm seated across from him again, he says,

"You did it."

"What?" I say.

"You're out. You made it."

"You mean I won't be drafted?"

"You'll get a new card with your changed status in the mail."

I'm unable to move or say anything.

"You're free to go," the officer says.

I want to thank him but am afraid that if I say anything I'll find out it's some kind of trap.

My car is at my parents' house. I catch a bus at the Greyhound station downtown. It would have been easier to drive to the induction center from my apartment in Seattle this morning, but they made me spend last night at the YMCA with the other inductees. The Greyhound lets me off on the highway, and as I walk up the hill, his car passes me, then stops.

"How did it go?" my father asks.

"Good," I say. "I flunked."

As I expected, he's upset. For him, the war in Vietnam can't be just a civil war or an attempt to overthrow a corrupt government. It's part of a Devil-driven, Communist plot to take over the world. If we don't stop them, they'll soon be here.

My father seemed to need to prove that his commitment to God was unconditional and true. As his son, I was included in that commitment. If he failed to deliver me as equally committed to the cause as he was, he was failing God. His generation has been called the Greatest Generation because they made sacrifices to check the advances of some very dangerous powers. Without World War II, I would not have been born. His time in the army was the highlight of his life. He met my mother during that time. But he was never in combat and spent the war guarding the Boeing aircraft plant in Seattle.

I was supposed to believe that once the Communist Chinese-supported North Vietnamese conquered South Vietnam, they would keep coming. Thailand, Cambodia and Laos would be next, then Burma, Africa, and Seattle. By going to Vietnam and killing *gooks*, I was supposed to be protecting my mother, my sisters, my little brothers, my neighbors, and my now ex-wife.

The terror of sweeping Communism drove American political leaders into sending people my age to the other side of the world to kill and be killed. My generation had mixed feelings about buying into the terror of our parents' generation. Arthur Miller, whose play, *The Crucible*, uses the Salem witch trials to illuminate the McCarthy Period and the dangerous place runaway fear can lead, said, "What terrifies one generation is likely to bring only a puzzled smile to the next." He also said, "Fear doesn't travel well; just as it can warp judgment, its absence can diminish memory's truth."

"It's because of my back," I say, trying to break the awkward silence.

My father doesn't say anything, and we're both quiet the rest of the way to the house. As we get out of the car, I say,

"My divorce was final on Monday."

"Oh?" my father says. "I'm sorry."

My mother is setting the table for dinner. "This is a surprise," she says. "What does it mean?"

"I don't have to go because of my back," I say.

"Thank God!" she says. "Can you stay for dinner? We've got plenty."

My youngest brother, David, who's fourteen, comes in from the backyard. When my father is about to pray, there's still an empty place setting and we hear a loud motorcycle in the driveway.

Mark, my other brother, who's nineteen, still lives at home and hasn't yet joined a commune or changed his name to Daniel, puts his helmet and gloves on the floor in the corner and says,

"I see you still have all your hair. Did they get you?"

"They don't want me."

"I'll bet that broke your heart."

"About like when you heard your lottery number."

"Sit down," our mother says. "You can wash up after we pray."

When we're eating, my youngest brother asks, "What was it like?"

"A lot of tests."

"Did they make you strip for your physical?"

"No," I say. "I guess they believed the letter from the doctor."

" Would you have gone?"

"I don't know," I say. "I don't think so."

"Would you have gone to jail or to Canada?"

"Probably jail."

"Why wouldn't you go?"

"It's a civil war between the Vietnamese. It's not our war."

"What if the Communists come here?"

"We used to live on a commune. Communism is just a different way of distributing stuff. It's an economic system, like capitalism. It isn't always a plot to take over the world."

"That's enough!" my father says. "Your brothers are still my sons. This is still my house, and I won't have you coming here and poisoning their minds."

They're all looking at me. I say, "You're right. It's your house. If I'm not welcome here, I'll leave and I won't come anymore."

Twelve

Our tour guide in Vietnam was born the year the war ended. He chose not to have us attempt to pronounce his real name. Instead we called him "Johnny." In the new air-conditioned bus that brought our tour group to Củ Chi from a four-star hotel in old Saigon (now thought of as a district in the modern, much larger Ho Chi Min City) he told us that Vietnam has struggled with foreign occupation or been at war for most of the past thousand years.

According to Johnny, the Vietnamese feel they were used as pawns in a bigger international power struggle that included China and Russia. They now believe that the Americans waged war with good intentions based on false assumptions.

When Johnny gets to his personal story, I see emotion welling up, and there are moments when it's clear he's pulling himself together, struggling to keep his composure. I'm not the only one with father issues. His father was a Viet Cong, and when he didn't come home after the war, they thought he was dead. He showed up a few years later, emotionally unbalanced and drinking heavily, and made life difficult for the family. Eventually he was diagnosed with PTSD and got treatment. He was able to connect with some American soldiers he fought against, and since then, the family has had a better life. I'm guessing Johnny's father and the American soldiers got to see in each other's eyes the same pain and vulnerability I saw in my father's eyes the second time I hit him. His father's status as a war veteran helped Johnny obtain his education.

Besides sightseeing in Ho Chi Minh City, Hanoi and Da Nang, the Vietnam portion of our trip included visits to several beautiful temples, and in Hue, we toured The Citadel. One can't help but be impressed by huge structures that required monumental organization and the intricate coordination of resources to build.

Our greatest temple exposure came in Cambodia where Angkor Wat transcends even Hue's Imperial City. In the twelfth century, King Suryavarman II had Angkor Wat built on a 400-acre site near what is now the city of Seam Reap. Angkor Wat started out as a state temple to the Hindu god, Vishnu. The structure was also intended as the eventual mausoleum for the king. After Suryavarman's death, it was transformed into a Buddhist temple. Between five and ten million sandstone blocks weighing up to 1.5 tons each had to be moved from quarries twenty-five miles away. Presumably, elephants helped, but the amount of human labor involved had to be enormous. I can't help but imagine a workforce of individuals whose lives didn't matter to the rulers coerced into backbreaking, dangerous labor.

We were told by our Cambodian guide that Suryavarman was attempting to build "Heaven on Earth." In 1970, twenty-five years after World War II ended and the summer before I flunked my draft physical, I found myself standing in a gas chamber at the Dachau death camp in Germany, looking at a tool used by the Nazis in their attempt to create their supremacist version of "Heaven on Earth."

A college kid spending the summer in Europe was probably more common then than it is now. For this kid, it was unreal. At the time, I was barely an adult, and the world I had been trying to piece together had crumbled. I had done my best and failed. I lived day-to-day, hoping something good would happen. I had decided to finish the year at school, get in my old VW bug, take the little money I had and leave Seattle, go somewhere, anywhere.

At the end of an earlier term, when I couldn't get the course-work for his class done, my Shakespeare professor gave me an extension. He seemed sympathetic. I was desperate, so I went to him again and told him about my marriage, how it was breaking up and how my life was falling apart. He was taking his family to England for a year on a teaching exchange. He's told me since that he was convinced I wouldn't be alive when he got back, so he loaned me money, bought me more days to find hope, pulled me out of my narrow world, and sent me on an adventure. The loan covered a school-sponsored charter flight to London and left me with enough to buy food and stay in hostels. So instead of wandering alone in the States, I was wandering Europe alone, but with a safety valve. Because I knew I was welcome, over the summer I was drawn several times back to London and the house his family rented there.

My memory of the room at Dachau is that it was bare gray cement, but there might have been flaking paint on the ceiling. On each wall there was a different life-sized picture from when it was in operation. Naked people were herded into the room. Pictures showed the anguish and terror as they realized they were being gassed, bodies on the floor, bodies being dragged through the door to the furnaces. The room wasn't huge, but stark, ugly in its raw practicality. The pipes protruding from the ceiling with supposed showerheads gave the space an industrial, boiler-room feel. The crematorium and furnaces outside cut through any sense of denial or protective distance. The spirits of the dead were still on watch. A feeling in the air made the immediacy of the horror palpable.

Without all those people we see cheering him on in the old movies of his rallies, Hitler couldn't have been Hitler. It took people to do the herding, the locking of doors, the opening of gas valves and the dragging of bodies. Each had crossed a line, made a choice.

In the laundry room there are shelves along the back wall, and as I take down my boxes of things I couldn't face to sort—high school yearbooks, wedding pictures, mortgage papers, my old baseball glove—I line them up on the floor near the workbench. I hear the door at the top of the stairs close, then feel his hand on my shoulder.

"Wait," my father says.

"What for?"

"I want to talk to you."

It's hard to look at him. I say, "There's nothing to say. You're right. It's your house and you don't want me here, so I'm leaving."

"I don't want you to leave," he says.

"You don't like anything about me."

"You're my son." His voice falters. "I love you."

He puts his arms around me and hugs me. His body is close and his arms are confining and make me uncomfortable. "But you don't like anything about me," I say again.

"You're my son. You came from me."

My father is crying. I can't say that I love him back or move to return his hug.

"You have to understand," he says, "that I'm a man and I've put a lot of thought into what I believe and think is right. This is my house and your brothers still live here and are my responsibility. As long as I have any influence, I can't allow you or anyone else to come here and say things that go against everything I believe."

"I'm a man, too," I say, "and I've put a lot of thought into what I believe. They're my brothers and I can't lie to them or you about what I think just because I know it will upset you."

My father looks at me for a long time. "I don't want to fight with you," he says.

I look at the boxes. I recognize in his voice the desperation of knowing you need to fix something, but are only making it worse.

"I want you to feel welcome here," he says. "I want you to feel that

this is a place for you to come when you need friends, but I have to ask you to respect my beliefs in my house."

"What I believe means as much to me as what you believe does to you."

"Can we shake hands and go up and finish dinner?" my father asks.

Finally, I offer my hand.

The My Lai Massacre happened in March of 1968. In 1971, *The New York Times* published *The Pentagon Papers*, revealing that the Johnson administration had systematically lied to the American public and to Congress about the war that my father still believed in. I flunked my draft physical in the spring of 1971 and wasn't forced to choose.

I went to Vietnam partly to see what had grown out of the horror I escaped. In *The Zenith*, writer Duong Thu Huong has the Ho Chi Minh-based character, the President, say, "Liberation is meaningless if it does not make people happier. All revolutions are crazy and cruel games, should they fail to bring freedom and a worthy life. It is the same with independence. Independence is valueless if the people of an independent country do not find themselves able to stand on their own two feet as far as the most essential necessities are concerned."

My father's path toward happiness and a meaningful life didn't ring true for me. In Vietnam, our tour guide described American involvement as well-meant but misguided. I would describe my father's attempts at intervention in my life, my coming of age, the same way.

In Hanoi, besides visiting the "Hanoi Hilton" where American POWs were imprisoned, we toured Ba Dinh Square where Ho Chi Minh's mausoleum is located. Ho Chi Minh is an adopted name meaning "Bringer of Light." Ho was born in 1890 when Vietnam was part of French Indochina. He founded the Indochinese Communist Party in 1930, and led the Vietnamese independence movement from 1941 until his death in 1969. He died before his country won victory over the Americans and became united under Communist rule. The first years of independence after America pulled its troops out were hard years in Vietnam.

Ho continues to be a symbol. In the heavily guarded, air-conditioned, central hall, Ho's preserved body is encased in glass. The display was inspired by Lenin's tomb. After depositing cameras, phones and packs, and waiting in a long line, we were allowed to file by. No sign of disrespect allowed—no crossing of arms, hands in pockets, eating, photos, or smoking.

Ho was presented as monk-like in his dedication and his sacrifice of any kind of personal life or gratification that might get in the way of the pursuit of his ideals. His persona is tied to his commitment to the cause. In the last years of his life, Ho got pushed out of frontline decision-making and was under what amounted to house arrest.

Writer Duong Thu Huong claims that Ho had a young mistress who bore him two children, and that party officials were so afraid that his saint-like image would be tarnished that they had her murdered, clubbed to death and dumped by the side of the road as the victim of a fake traffic accident. The choices we make, even when they are driven by high ideals, are also driven by our own needs. Whether it involves a single child or a country, governing is complicated (to say the least).

I'm sure Ho Chi Minh loved his country and his mistress. I also believe my father's love for me was real and I know that my love for him was. Our relationship was complicated by unresolvable differences, but I know we were both better off than we would have been had my father not come to the basement and offered his hand that night after I was turned down by the draft.

Thirteen

Passion is a mysterious thing.

When my son was young, preschool age, he had a fixation on cattails. He loved them. He would get excited when, from the car, he saw some on the side of the road. One of my most salient father-of-young-boy memories is of taking him in our small outboard skiff up a slough at the mouth of the river into cattail heaven. The cattails were at the perfect stage in their cycle, the cylindrical brown seedpods still tight. They surrounded us, and his delight and excitement were thrilling. He was having that experience fathers undergo great effort to provide for their children, and frequently fail. All I did was recognize his passion and deliver him to the place that would fulfill it. We picked as many as he wanted and he kept them in his room until the pods started to disintegrate, their released fluff making a serious mess. The passion for cattails eventually faded and finally disappeared. I have no idea where it came from or why it left, but I am glad he's found new ones that work for him.

My passion for boats and water is not quite as mysterious to me as my son's attraction to cattails. My grandfather was a sea captain. Pictures of him and stories about him were embedded in the time I spent with my grandmother at her house on the beach, though it was not from her that I learned he used *the gun* and died just before I was born rather than remain bedridden, debilitated by a stroke.

When I was seven, our family made a trip to Alaska on a power scow, stopping at Native villages. We were the supply boat following a small ship that delivered doctors and dentists who stayed, treating the villagers, for a week. I was happy on that trip and have clear memories of it. Rocky shorelines, eagles, whales and dolphins, the smell of diesel-soaked wood and the feel of moving over big water, all found a place in my store of memories. They never left me and have drawn me with a power that rivaled the draw of the dark broody place I went for control and safety when I felt powerless.

Allie and I had been together for half a year. After living together for three months, we had gotten married on the sly, by a judge in the courthouse. The crash happened on Saturday, around noon. The day was sunny and I was heading home on a small Yamaha I had bought from a neighbor. Traffic was light, but I was behind a cluster of four or five cars. There were no cars behind me. Suddenly, a blue Oldsmobile heading the opposite direction turned across my lane in front of me.

In the flash of a second, I understood there was no way to avoid collision. I envisioned splat. I was done, and believed it in my core. I have no memory of the impact, but remember gray, then surprise at the crunch sound of my helmet hitting cement, and more surprise when I found myself under a rhododendron bush, conscious. There was no helmet law then, and I usually didn't wear one. It came with the bike and I had taken it off the hook as I grabbed my jacket, as a kind of afterthought. Allie cared about me; I should think about safety.

People working in their yards saw the crash. I remember a man calming me, persuading me to stay still, telling me the Oldsmobile driver had stopped and the police were on their way. A lady got my phone number from my wallet, called Allie and described seeing me go over the top of the car, then said I was being taken to the hospital in an ambulance. The lady didn't know if I was badly hurt.

Allie arrived at the emergency room shortly after I did. It turned out most of the damage was to my right kneecap. The wound was pretty ugly with exposed bone, muscle and tendon. Because my helmet was cracked, they worried about brain damage and couldn't put me out. Allie stayed beside the bed, between the doctors and me, blocking my view while they operated. They used a local anesthetic, but I could hear and feel what they were doing. The pain was severe and Allie did her best to keep me distracted.

The defining decisions in my life have been driven by a combination of a need to escape something and passions that were unclear but drew me to specific places. Teachers and books had been instrumental in helping me stay a step ahead of despair. When I managed to stay in college, I had to declare a major. I chose English/Education. It covered the reading that I loved and presented the possibility that I could become like the people in my life who had seen past my anger and grief into something of value inside me that I couldn't acknowledge or develop alone. Because they saw it and responded to it, I had been able to find a way to own some of it too. Maybe I could do that for someone else.

During my junior and senior years of college, I experienced day-to-day life as an emotional war zone. I felt that I was navigating a minefield. When I graduated, I was nowhere near ready to stand in front of a class of high school students. It became clear to me that I couldn't complete the education sequence needed to get a teaching certificate. I found comfort in stories about other people who felt disconnected. In junior high, *Catcher in the Rye* had a profound affect on me. Later, Camus' *The Stranger* struck a sensitive chord. I was obsessed with writers and envied their ability to connect by reflecting life back through stories that rang true.

At that time, the University of Washington was one of only a few schools that offered an English degree with a writing curriculum, and I opted for it. While my writing wasn't good enough to validate my dreams of being a writer, it was good therapy. It was composed, as my father recognized, of thinly disguised accounts of my life. I now recognize it as a form of meditation that helped me understand and clarify my own story.

I found a job where I could write for a good cause while I tried to improve.

Like Vietnam, the Civil Rights Movement was affecting my life and had become personal, but my getting involved was accidental. My sister, Lilly, had fallen in love with a black man. They had a young daughter, and their relationship had brought out the dark side of my father, so my sister and I became allies. In the fall of 1969, as I began my junior year at the University of Washington, a listing that included writing appeared as a Work Study job option. It was a paid internship at the local branch of a national civil rights organization.

I looked up what they did. Their mission included integration. I took a chance, and applied. Besides my father's reaction to my sister's relationship, my then wife's mother had also married a black man. When he moved into the house on a suburban Snohomish County cul-de-sac, friends of the two younger girls still living at home were no longer allowed to visit. "For Sale" signs went up for neighboring houses. Eventually the family moved to an integrated neighborhood in Oakland. I described these experiences during my interview and they hired me.

The first year I wrote some pamphlets, and listened a lot. As the trial separation in my marriage became permanent, the people at work were good to me, treating me as family. I spent more time at my sister's apartment where my disconsolate moods were tempered by kindness. But I was struggling, and by the end of the year, when my professor offered the Europe option, I was in a pretty dark place. He may well have been right about how close I was to doing something drastic.

When I returned from my summer in Europe, the civil rights organization took me back, and when I flunked my draft physical and graduated, they created a salaried position for me. Though my personal life was a mess, at work I felt like I belonged. I met Allie the week after I flunked my draft physical. Even though there were red flags that made her keep her distance at first, she must have seen something in me that piqued her interest. I was connecting with people and beginning to heal.

My job was political. To do it well required passion and commitment. It offered a unique opportunity to advance in Seattle politics, and I was making connections but found myself unprepared to take the path that was opening in front of me. I felt that I was wasting an opportunity. The right person, preferably a black person, could put the position to much better use. My office had a view of the harbor, and I found myself watching ships and tugboats come and go.

Riding home on my motorbike that sunny morning, at the moment of recognition that impact was inevitable, my belief that I would die was certain. It couldn't have been more than a few seconds before the sound of my helmet hitting the curb brought me back, but it seemed forever. The wreck didn't, as cancer would later, make the dark moods go away, but it reoriented the way I approached and experienced life. It altered the context of risk.

Allie and I lived in Seattle's University District near the north shore of Lake Union. As therapy for my damaged knee, I rode a bicycle and used my exercise excursions to take in the houseboats, pleasure boat marinas and commercial docks that lined the lake's edge. There was a for-sale sign on an old wooden tugboat moored at one of the docks. I suppose it was my memory of the Alaska trip that drew me. The gate to the dock was open, so I parked the bicycle and had a look.

The marina attendant treated me like a potential buyer, which surprised me. He gave me a serious tour. It was a small ship that could take you to Alaska. There were staterooms and a galley. You could live on it. Walking the decks, I was captivated. Standing at the wheel in the pilothouse, smelling the diesel-soaked wood of the spacious engine room with twin engines in line, driving a single propeller shaft, made an impression on me. For something that substantial, the price seemed low. I didn't understand yet that because it was made of wood, even though it was still functional, maintenance was prohibitive, and like the ships that had been burned at Richmond beach, it was obsolete. But it got me thinking about boats and I scanned boat listings in the newspaper want ads.

I can't remember the details of the transition, but it involved funding cuts at work that didn't specifically affect my job, but made me feel wrong for continuing to occupy a spot that someone else could take better advantage of. I had paid down the medical debt and, after a bad experience with a renter, sold the house from my first marriage for more than we paid. I used that money and the insurance settlement from the motorbike wreck and borrowed money from my professor friend to buy an old wooden tugboat, much smaller than the one that originally caught my eye.

I quit my job.

Fourteen

It was 1972. Seattle still had the feel of the sixties. The war in Vietnam continued with no end in sight. The first major gas crisis would come a year later. People my age were challenging the old ways, challenging accepted career paths, joining communes. Puget Sound had been ever-present in my life. In college, when I was short of money, I supplemented my diet with fish and crab I caught snorkeling. Water and boats were everywhere. Fishing was still a viable way to earn a living. Young people I knew who had bought commercial licenses and old wooden boats seemed to be making it. They were self-employed, taking their living from nature.

Following a similar dream with a tugboat didn't seem that far-fetched. Murray Morgan, in his book, *The Last Wilderness*, about early days on the Olympic Peninsula, describes a couple who made their living salvaging and selling logs that had escaped from booms being towed in Puget Sound. You could get a Log Patrol license from the state, and there were still a few people doing it.

Believing it was somehow in my blood and drawn to it the way my son was to cattails, I dove in blind. I had no idea what I was getting into and where it might lead, but Allie was up for the adventure, so off the cliff we jumped. We should have failed miserably, and without support from friends, especially the professor, we would have.

To my surprise, my father liked the boat. He didn't think I was crazy and didn't complain when I postponed repaying the

money I had borrowed from my mother to buy the house until
the insurance settlement came. The boat became part of our narrow strip of common ground, a new way to have a conversation
without anxiety.

I secured a Log Patrol license and a license to fish for Dungeness
crab. Maybe between the two, I could make a go of it. The crab
license allowed me to get cheap moorage at Fisherman's Terminal in Ballard. I bought some used crab gear and a towline, and
worked at getting to know the boat. Lee Miller, the brother of my
upstairs neighbor, was between jobs and intrigued enough by the
adventure of it to help. He had much more mechanical and practical experience than I had, and without him, everything would
have played out differently.

Logs are branded like cattle were in the old west. The Log
Patrol license allowed us to retrieve branded logs off any beach.
When I thought we were ready, I rented a berth at Cape Sante
marina and made the voyage to Anacortes, the twelve-foot aluminum boat loaned by my father secured on deck. There was a
log yard on Guemes Channel that would store and sell our logs.
The brand holder would get a share but we would get most of
the money. We were assigned a spot in the yard's protected cove
and assured that the logs we put there would be recorded in our
account.

The work was hard, dangerous but fun, and we actually found
some logs on our first outing. We got the towline tangled in the
propeller only once. I had to get in the water to clear it before
the boat went aground. On the way back to town, we added a
bundle we found floating to the logs we had pulled off the beach.
We discovered that towing logs was a slow process that required
calm water and favorable current. The little tug had a World War
II-vintage diesel engine, sixty horsepower, more power than the
original 1927 engine, but inadequate for even a small tugboat to-

day. The Mussel needed more muscle. When we finally secured our first tow at the log yard, we felt pretty good.

But when we went in on Monday to check, the logs were gone and the yard claimed they knew nothing about them. They were polite, but clear, they had no evidence of any logs being delivered over the weekend. I was upset but had way too much invested to see what should have been plain. Someone didn't want us here. We headed across Rosario Straight to the San Juan Islands. If nothing else it would be a way to get to know the area, and maybe we would find logs.

The islands are beautiful. In a strange way, cruising among them, absorbing the gray mood of rocky, tree-lined shores felt like going home. It reconnected me with images and memories of the Alaska trip. We spent the night at the guest dock in Friday Harbor. On our way to Roche Harbor the next day, we went close to the Spieden Island shore. The island had been populated with exotic game animals and for a rich-person fee, you could hunt for trophy there. Through the binoculars, the animals we saw looked like sheep. We tied up in Roche Harbor and explored the town before resuming our search for logs.

The south shore of John's Island looked like it might have potential, and we crossed over for a closer look. On the chart there were two asterisks indicating rocks close together at about the middle of the long stretch of beach. The depth there went from more than six fathoms to one-and-a-half. I had bought a fathometer and was keeping an eye on it. Confident that we were out beyond the rocks, our attention was focused on looking through the binoculars for salvageable logs.

When we hit, the boat lurched, raised up and stopped moving. The propeller was still submerged and hadn't struck anything. The engine strained. I remember disbelief, shock, shifting to reverse to no avail, then going out on deck and seeing through the shallow water the mussels and seaweed on what turned out to be

the top of a big rock. Had we been only a few yards farther away
from shore, we would have missed it. We checked for leaks, then
checked the tide book. The tide was going out. We were stuck.

The Mussel wasn't designed to go aground safely. It had a
narrow, deep, and very sturdy hull. It was overbuilt, designed to
herd logs. The keel was made from substantial timbers and the
planking was equivalent to what would be used on a boat twice
its size. But because it was narrow and deep, unless it was floating or supported with something to hold it upright, it would lie
on its side. As the water level dropped, it did just that, but luckily
it tipped toward the main mass of rock and settled, listing severe-
ly, into a tilted perch on the pinnacle.

It was clear that when the tide came in the hull would fill if we
didn't do something. We launched the skiff to have it ready and
reported our situation to the Coast Guard. They sent a helicopter
from Port Angeles and told us the cutter that was on its way from
Anacortes would take a few hours to get to us. We had some tubes
of caulking with us, and some nails. We used plywood from the
bulkhead between the engine compartment and the bunk space
to cover the two windows on the down side and caulked as best
we could to slow the influx of water when the tide came back up.
Then we got in the skiff and headed for the beach to wait.

From the skiff, the Mussel, perched in the air above the water, lying on its side, bow and stern extended beyond the supporting jut of rock, looked to me like a giant trophy celebrating
failure. We sat on a log and let the devastation sink in. It's a nice
beach. Lee has a great sense of humor and tried to distract me by
making jokes. The Coast Guard boat arrived and stood by as the
tide came in. Their mission was to save us if we were in danger
of drowning and to assess any environmental damage or hazard
to navigation caused by our mishap. We were in no immediate
danger, but we were stranded. Our skiff wouldn't get us home,
and something needed to be done with the Mussel.

Since we had found no serious damage to the hull, the cutter crew decided to use us as a training opportunity. The tow bit on the Mussel was located just aft of the pilothouse about halfway between the stern and bow. They secured a towline to it allowing the cutter to take a strain athwart ship away from the rock toward deeper water, coaxing the hull upright as the tide came in. They loaned us a gas-powered pump. The trick was to keep enough water out of the hull to enable us to float. Keeping the hull as upright as possible allowed less water in, but, given the size and power of the cutter, there was the risk of accidentally pulling too hard and capsizing toward deep water. We found the right balance and were able to refloat.

The cutter towed us back to Anacortes.

The Mussel was forty-six years old, a relic from the past. Looking back with what I learned later, I realized I could have flushed the water out of the base of the engine, caulked a few seams and put the boat back in the water. I would have been back where I was before the big event. But I would have had to face the impracticality of my dream, rethink my way forward.

With the keel safely resting on blocks, the hull held upright by four fifty-five gallon oil drums, I drove home, still in my wetsuit. There was no shower in the U-District apartment, so I was in the bathtub when the phone rang. The woman on the other end told me my name had come to the top of the waiting list for the mechanic training program at the city's technical college. I had called them to enquire about an engine repair class and been told all the classes were part of a two-year program. Even though I wasn't interested in enrolling in the entire program, she had put my name on the waiting list.

Classes had just started and the person on the phone said someone had dropped out. She was trying to fill the spot and my name had come to the top. If I was interested, I needed to start tomorrow. There I was, wet and naked under a bath towel, my broken boat in the boatyard with water in the engine and me knowing almost nothing about fixing it. A phone call at a key moment altered the course of my life. I said yes.

Fifteen

The next day, I went to what turned out to be a welding class. My first experience with a cutting torch was transformative. It amazed me. I had watched my father struggle with metal objects enough to consider them formidable. I learned you could cut that stuff like butter. Then you could fuse it together any way you chose. You could order steel cut to size and make things out of it, like a wood stove or a new tugboat rudder.

My neighbor at that time had written but not turned in his PhD thesis. He was reconsidering academic life. He took a job driving a Seattle transit bus as a way to get closer to the way normal people lived. Driving a bus is a transferrable skill. There are busses and trucks moving things everywhere, and if you are comfortable with it, a skill like that will allow you a valuable kind of internal freedom, freedom to think and not to feel that you were trading your soul for money. I rode my neighbor's bus run and considered what he was doing.

It occurred to me that there was machinery everywhere, owned mostly by people who depend on it but don't know how to fix it. I was fascinated by what I was learning at mechanic school. I knew that technical writing, even for a cause I believed in, hadn't been my answer. The dark place inside me wasn't far beneath the surface. Allie's support and friendship, her upbeat attitude, kept me happy most of the time, but my mental state was still volatile. I liked working with my hands, found myself drawn to mechanical puzzles, and was driven to prove that I could solve them. Like writing, it was good therapy. By the end of ten weeks of welding,

I was hooked.

I think people around me wondered what I was doing, borrowing money to go to a tech program for diesel mechanics when I already had a college degree. Why had I quit my writing job? Why hadn't I found another, similar position? My obsession with tugboats hadn't gone away. Troubleshooting and solving mechanical logic problems built up my self-confidence.

Also, it had become apparent that the emergency room surgery hadn't fixed the injured leg from the motorbike crash. I could walk and do most things. I could function at school and work on the boat, but my leg wasn't healing right. After a painful year and a half, there was a severe flare-up and they had to operate again. The second try worked. School seemed as good a place as any to be while I was recovering. Owning an old wooden boat gave what I was learning at school a purpose, and we managed to keep the sense of adventure alive.

Looking back, had we not run the boat aground, I likely would have come around to accept that I was in over my head, found a buyer for the boat, and moved on with my life. I can't say what that failure would have done to my mental state, but I would not have said yes when the woman from the tech program called.

When I bought the Mussel, there was no license required to operate a towboat, even a big one, and when we went on our ill-fated, log-salvage excursions, we could legally pull logs from beaches and tow them to the log yard. I could do whatever other towing jobs I could find, but I soon discovered that a new law would require operators of tugboats over twenty-six feet long to be licensed. If you could prove that you had run a tugboat for a specified amount of time, and pass a navigation rules test, you were grandfathered in. Otherwise, you had to go through an apprenticeship, meaning you had to accrue sea time on a working boat before you could sit for a comprehensive exam.

Even if the Mussel had not been in the boatyard on blocks, it's unlikely that I would have logged the necessary working time to be grandfathered before the window closed. If I wanted to follow my tugboat captain dream, I would need to get a job on someone else's boat, acquire the sea time and pass the exam. I privately identified myself as a writer and this was my way of getting material, living real life. I was having an adventure, my Jack London phase. The mechanic classes I was taking were interesting and challenging, and meshed well with my tugboat fantasy. I focused on what I was being taught, and it gave me purpose while my leg was healing.

Lee Miller and I overhauled the Mussel's old engine. I found a wooden-boat repair shop in an old waterfront warehouse on the channel. They were busy refurbishing a power scow similar to the one that, as a child, I had ridden to Alaska. They agreed to do the work I couldn't on the Mussel and let us moor the boat there. What may have been more important, in exchange for welding and engine work, they coached me through work on the Mussel we thought I could tackle on my own and let me use their tools. I got to apply what I was learning about engines, hydraulic systems and wiring to boats while adding woodworking skills.

They allowed Allie and me to spend weekends and days off in the living quarters on the power scow. We fell in love with the town and the surrounding area. Allie got bored with too much technical boat stuff, but the adventure of cooking and sleeping on a boat and exploring a new place sustained her patience through hours of boat talk that, for me, was like an extension of mechanic school.

She was working at a photo finishing company in Seattle and had laid prints from a freshly developed roll of Mussel pictures on the counter during a lull in customers. The guy who came through the door was a regular who brought in film of damaged cargo from his company for insurance claims. He asked about the tugboat pictures on the counter and revealed that besides trucks, his company had tugboats. In the conversation that followed, Allie told him I was looking for a job on a boat. He ended up giving her his work phone number with an invitation for me to call.

The interview went well, but there was no immediate opening for an engineer or deckhand. As I was leaving I was asked if I could cook. Though my skill was very limited, I said yes and was offered a week's work as a relief cook. On the way home I bought a cookbook and spent the days before I was to sail figuring out recipes, practicing. After more relief work, I was hired. We rented a house in the town on the channel where the Mussel was moored and moved there.

During a lay-off caused by a Canadian pulp-and-paper-workers' strike, I took a summer job on a purse seiner. I had completed six of the eight terms needed for a certificate from the diesel program. We fished in Southeast Alaska, and in another curious turn of events, I was able to get my certificate from the diesel school.

I was on a good boat, but it was a bad year with few fish to catch, and late in the season, the cannery sent many of the workers home. Then there was a run of fish, and my captain, who had recruited his daughters, offered to have Allie fly up with them. She could work in the cannery for a few weeks, sharing cannery housing with the two high-school-age girls, then ride home on the boat with us. She jumped at the opportunity.

During the slow times between fishing days, I worked in the cannery's mechanic shop. When boats were finally catching fish, bad weather had hit. Some seine skiffs had gotten swamped while running, and I had the engine of one of them apart on a table. I was putting it back together, replacing the damaged parts, when I felt someone watching. The familiar face was a complete surprise. One of the instructors from my mechanic program was working upstairs in the cannery as a supervisor. It was a way for him to make some extra money and spend a little time in Alaska where, even in a bad year, the sports fishing is much better than in Puget Sound. He was Allie's boss.

Allie had told him about my tugboat job and the lay-off and how we ended up here. He talked to my shop foreman and told me that because I was working in the industry at a job I had trained for at school, I could apply for a waiver and maybe get my mechanic certificate. The two terms I had missed were all shop classes where you were assigned a variety of troubleshooting and repair jobs, testing whether you could put what you had learned to use. It was exactly what I was doing in the cannery shop and on the Mussel at home. He agreed to vouch for me. When I got home, I applied for the waiver and the diploma came in the mail.

The pulp-and-paper-workers' strike ended and I went back on the tugs. Sometimes I was the cook and sometimes a deckhand/engineer and eventually I logged enough time to sit for my Operator's License exam. It hadn't taken long for me to realize that even now, self-employed and with a captain's license, scrounging for work on my own little boat, running crab pots in season and repairing fishing boat engines, all of this would not compare favorably with working a union job on a big tug.

In my time at home, I'd learned that I wasn't a great businessman. I enjoyed getting to know the fishermen, and it felt good to be valued when I could help them out with mechanical problems, but I lacked the confidence to charge enough to live comfortably. The tugboat company seemed to value me. It was family-owned and because we also worked cargo in home ports, the normal crew hierarchy was less rigid. We were a team and covered for each other. At that time, we still worked two weeks on and two weeks off, so my time home was predictable. We had enough money. Allie had good friends nearby and didn't need to have a job unless she wanted one. She could go to school.

A few months after I got my Operator's License, I was on a boat towing a loaded barge back to Seattle. A call came on the radio and I was instructed to have my gear ready to shift when we docked. The company had finally bought the boat for a new run to the west coast of Vancouver Island. As part of the purchase agreement, in order to facilitate my transfer to chief engineer, a man who had worked the new (to us; built in 1941) boat was hired to train me, and I made the transition into my new job.

After we got home from the fishing adventure in Alaska, Allie and I were able to buy the house we were renting. A few years later, we decided to be brave, and our daughter was born. Our situation with my absence wasn't unique in the fishing, farming and tugboat town where we lived. Many of my crewmates also lived there. Allie had befriended another tugboat widow and found she could manage in my absence.

My absence was hard on my kids, especially my daughter. When she was small, she could sense when I was about to leave. When I tried to help with something like tying her shoes or getting her coat on, she'd say, "Not you! I want Mom." When I came home she was happy, but within a day or two, there would be some condition she'd let me know about in some subtle way that I'd have to meet to merit her forgiveness.

The tugboat experience earned my father's respect in a way teaching never would have. As the boat's engineer, I was part of the team, but separate enough to avoid difficult personality conflicts. If I did my job well, I was left alone and treated with respect. The crazy idealism of my attempt at log salvage evolved into a career. I had time to read, time to write, and enough money that Allie could choose not to work if her job didn't allow her to put our kids first.

Sixteen

Allie and I are at our daughter's house. We have come to babysit our grandsons while their parents go on a date. My daughter hands me an envelope. It contains postcards I'd sent when she was a child, during my tugboat time. I park myself on the couch and flip through the cards.

Dear Emilie (and her mom),

There was a big storm when we crossed the Gulf of Alaska. It was a rough ride for a few days. We had to wait for a ship to be unloaded before we could tie up at the only dock available in Cordova. We went around in circles in a place called Orca Bay. I caught a salmon. One night we saw the Northern lights. It was beautiful. I'll be home as soon as I can.

Love, Dad

At the bottom of the engine room ladder, ear protection on but still in my skivvies, I'm relieved to see the expected oil level light glowing red on the panel. I hit the button, silencing the shrill wail from the World War II air-raid signal. The light flickers out for a moment, then, as the boat takes another roll, comes on again. I silence the siren again and signal a thumbs-up to the watch deckhand who has appeared at the top of the ladder. He disappears forward. I pull on my coveralls.

In rough weather, the oil in the main engine base sloshes and activates the alarm sensor. I open the necessary valves to add lube oil from the storage tank. While the pump is running, I check the dipstick repeatedly, timing with the motion of the boat to get an idea of the true level and fill it as full as I dare. The alarm stays silent while I make my log entry.

The sour smell from the bilges is diluted by the cool air from the blower above the front of the engine, but the stink still makes me queasy. I'm sweating freely and I wipe my forehead with the clean grease rag I keep in my hip pocket. I fart and head for my lifeline porthole at the top of the forward engine-room ladder.

With each swell, a torrent gushes along the deck between the bulwark and the house. Waves fold over the bulwarks and spray whips across the crests as the boat slogs ahead. The spray feels good on my face, but it's too late. After I throw up, as my dinner washes away, I spit to clear the taste from my mouth. For several minutes I breathe the cold, clean air and some steadiness comes back.

The wind has shifted direction. It's the mate's watch, and by adjusting our course to improve the ride, he's added miles to the trip. Yesterday afternoon the forecast for the week was good. It was sunny and clear when we pulled into the Gulf at Cape Spencer. La Peruse and the endless miles of mountains and other glaciers to our north were translucent green, stunning.

The ship is like a cocoon. This porthole connects me to the outer world. I'm poking my head out of this capsule that has been central to my orientation to the universe for at least half my days over the last several years. I'm hyper-aware of the familiar, self-contained space that insulates me from the emotional complexity of life in other places. Feeling protected by the boat around me, I center myself. I let the ocean touch me, affirm me.

The machine doesn't care about my emotions or what I believe. I monitor the systems, know the weak spots, and at any sign of trouble, attack the problem. Here I know my job. I'm part of a team. My role gives me purpose and connects me to a group of men living together in a box on the ocean, interdependent because we climb inside a piece of machinery, confront nature and together put ourselves at its mercy. It tests my ability to accurately read symptoms, think logically, diagnose and solve problems, sometimes before they occur. I need to be prepared with the right spare parts and tools. I'm the boat's immune system, the chief antibody.

I get to feel important, needed, and I get to take that home with me and be validated in my life on shore by what I do here. The struggle here is simple, narrowed by the challenge of staying alive and getting a job done without the confusion of trying to remain true to yourself, yet not disappoint. If we get there safely with our cargo, I've succeeded.

The elephant-gray mass of the engine dominates the two-story compartment behind me. At the level of the main deck, this boat has a catwalk like a balcony around the exhaust pipes and fresh air ducts above the engine. In boat language the space is called the *fiddley*. The catwalk's exterior bulkheads are lined with storage cabinets for spare parts and a back-up generator.

Before I return to bed for my two remaining off-watch hours, I go down the ladder to make a more thorough inspection. The engine room is a maze of electric motors, pumps, filter housings, plumbing and wiring, taking up at least half of the hull below deck. I keep it clean and almost everything is freshly painted. The open space around the engine and reduction gear is decked with diamond plate steel, painted burgundy. The deck plates are removable and beneath them are more wires and pipes, strainer housings and heat exchangers. The rest of the boat hull, ahead and aft of the engine room, is partitioned into fuel and water tanks, mostly fuel. This trip we're towing two big cargo barges, each more than twice the length of the boat and more than three times as wide, bound for Cordova and Kenai.

The EMD (General Motors Electromotive Division) engine is

much newer than the boat and came from a locomotive junkyard. We rebuilt it before installing it. Each of the sixteen pistons is the diameter of a large dinner plate. It's dependable and powerful, painted gray and designed to pull. Everything depends on it and it has karma you can sense. A big thundering heart surrounded by a lot of other organs. Nearly all the other machinery is World War II vintage, but it still does the job.

This boat is unique in that, instead of being on the after deck, the tow winch is mounted in the engine room behind the engine, above the propeller shaft. Having the tow winch in the engine room, out of the weather and dry, has kept it in excellent shape, and having its weight below the waterline improves the boat's stability. But since it isn't visible from the control station on the upper deck, whenever the winch is used someone has to be in the engine room. Communication is through a holler tube, its polished brass a reminder that the boat is a functioning antique.

I read the engine-monitoring gauges at the instrument panel, then circle the engine room, checking potential trouble spots, looking for oil or water leaks, or smoke, feeling for hot spots, sniffing for the unmistakable odor of overheated electrical insulation. Everything is normal. The bilge stink is normal for this boat. After dumping a few gallons of soap into the bilge water to sweeten the smell, I pat the forward valve cover the way you would pat a respected animal on the rump, and climb the ladder.

I must have dozed, because the rest of my off-watch bunk time passes quickly. From the motion of the boat, I sense that the wind has picked up. The swells are now big enough and far enough apart that the boat wants to surf down them. When a wave breaks over the stern, the bow is at the bottom of the trough digging into the next swell. Without the tow wire to stop it, the boat might broach sideways, but strain on the tow wire from the barges keeps the stern down, submerging the steering hydraulics and lifting the bow up, holding it in line.

The above-deck steering hydraulics were part of the upgrade that included replacing the engine. So far, the new tiller and cylinders, visible through the expanded metal panels of the low steel-framed poop deck, have worked. The swells wash knee-deep along the deck toward the bow. Luckily, as part of the refit, they replaced the big tire bumpers that would now be noisy and in danger of coming loose, with smooth, half-round, shock-absorbing rubber.

The boat rides like it's part submarine. The hull steel is fatigued from age and, as we're tossed, flexes just enough to allow seepage through door and porthole seals. Without the barges, we would have had to turn around and run slow into the wind to stay upright. Turning around in this swell would be dangerous.

I'm able to sleep a little during the afternoon and only have to get up once to tighten the winch brake. The amount of wire we string out between the tug and tow depends on the depth of the water, the weather and the load we're pulling. A quarter of a mile of cable separates us from the front barge, leaving only a wrap and a half of wire on the winch, not much if the brake doesn't hold. With this powerful wind behind us, dropping our speed to take pressure off the winch brake would risk losing control of the barges. By evening when I'm on watch again, conditions are worse.

The watch deckhand is seasick and the captain and I are the only ones up. My stomach has settled enough that I'm eating a ham sandwich and a cup of the chicken soup from the oversized pot the cook has secured with metal spring-wire bungees to the back corner of the oil stove. If I crush in enough soda crackers, maybe my stomach won't rebel. A big swell lifts the stern. I hang on to the dinette with one hand and the soup with the other. The boat shudders in a way I've never experienced, and my heart jumps. Through the galley's aft porthole it's too dark to see anything but turbulent water washing over the bulwarks. The vibration is short-lived, but I throw the food in the sink and run to the engine room.

All the gauges read normal and the engine seems fine. The winch brake is holding. I kneel on the catwalk over the reduction gear and look down on the turning propeller shaft. Nothing seems out of balance and I'm comforted that the vibration has stopped, making it unlikely that we have hit something with the propeller.

Back at my fiddley porthole, I see that the deck lights and the afterdeck floods are on. The swells are even bigger now, peaking far enough apart that when one lifts the stern and crests over it, the stern hangs out over the downslope at the back of the wave. The violent shudder might be from the top of the propeller catching air, creating cavitation. I watch, and when another big swell passes, the hull shakes again until the strain on the tow wire pulls the stern down.

The wave crest moves up the boat, putting the bulwarks completely under, passing only a foot or so below my porthole. I dog the porthole shut, go to the wheelhouse and tell the captain what I think. He experiments with the throttle, backing off just enough to soften the vibration and make it less frequent.

Halfway through the watch, I kneel on the catwalk above the reduction gear. The coupling that connects the propeller shaft to the reduction gear is spinning slowly enough to identify the bolts. Our lives depend on the huge five-bladed propeller at the end of the shaft, and on the rudder. Outside, the wind is now gusting at eighty knots and the waves are well over sixty feet high.

As the barges wallow in the swells, the strain on the tow wire increases and decreases and the engine governor adjusts fuel feed. I'm thinking about the surge chain that isn't between the end of the cable and the front barge. The surge chain is ninety feet long and each link weighs sixty pounds. It's above me, forward of the poop deck, looped in a big U on the stern. The crew spent considerable time securing it every few feet to the bulwark stanchions with heavy poly line. As we pitch and dive, I've been hearing it adjust position, testing the strength of the lashing lines.

There's a roar, like a ten-yard dump truck dropping a load of rocks on the deck plates above me!

The chain is loose!

I rush to the galley. The stern is completely awash. Chain soup! I imagine trying to secure it. Impossible! The big capstan is just aft of the house toward the starboard side and there's a huge cleat in the center of the deck-space for towing on a short, soft line. These two staunch deck fixtures are, for now, containing the chain's movement.

The roar of the engine momentarily fills the galley space as the door from the engine room opens and closes. The captain passes toward the other porthole; our eyes meet. His face is drained, as bloodless as mine feels. We watch the chain slide, our minds racing to find a way to avoid the eventual and inevitable breaching of the flimsy barrier that protects the steering hydraulics. When the steering goes, in a very short time the boat will be sideways in the swell. It will roll over and sink. We watch together in silence.

Would I have hooked the chain up, had the decision been mine? At Cape Spencer, the weather was beautiful. It's summer. I know the boat, have been through the hook-up process many times. I was relieved when he decided not to. Each barge has a towing bridle made of the same heavy chain with a forty-five-foot chain pennant that's connected to our tow cable. That's enough to absorb shock under normal sea conditions. This storm was not in the forecast.

The process of connecting the chain between the end of the towline and the barges is dangerous and the decision is not taken lightly. It must be done in calm water. The crew drags the chain by hand with steel hooks, spreading it into position, setting it up so that when the quick release is triggered, the chain doesn't catch on or damage anything in the few seconds it takes to fly overboard. The sound is deafening. Anything in the way gets mangled and taken over with it. The ancient capstan for hauling the chain back up barely has enough power, so at the end of the trip you have a dangerous disconnect procedure to deal with.

Now, instead of cushioning the tension on the wire with its weight, the three-ton shock absorber is loose on deck. Clumps of links slide forward when the bow dives, aft when the stern squats.

Neither of us moves. Eventually the mate joins us.

"I've got the crew ready," he says.

The captain shakes his head.

"Look out there," he says. "Even if we had harnesses to keep the guys from going overboard, you couldn't do anything. Our only hope would be to get an end started through a scupper and they've all got steel bars welded across them to keep loose lines from slipping through. It would likely hit the propeller." I let the mate have my porthole. He watches as the stern completely disappears under water with the peaking of each swell. We can hear but not see the chain shifting.

The mate goes back to the pilothouse. The captain and I watch our fate playing out in slow motion, waiting for the decisive moment when the chain breaks through and destroys the steering. We're silently orchestrating our next move – gathering the crew, calling the Mayday on the radio, donning survival suits, getting the life raft to the downwind side and launched, getting the crew in it before the boat rolls.

We're thirty miles offshore. A place called Dry Bay is the nearest point of reference on land. There's no harbor there. The Coast Guard might be able to get to us with a helicopter, but it would be a dangerous rescue.

"Look!" the captain says. "I don't fucking believe this!"

The stern lifts and the water is draining. The chain reveals itself in two tangles, one around the base of the capstan-shaft housing and the other around the big cleat in the center of the deck. There are two strands of chain running between the two tangles. They continue to slide noisily, but they're securely tangled, harmless to the steering.

Looking for permission to prepare for the inevitable jump-ship moment, a deckhand comes down. I give him my porthole and watch him understand the reprieve. Crew members take turns watching silently and it takes at least half an hour for belief to settle in.

Later, in the darkness of the pilothouse, the pale green glow of the radar cursor sweeping the screen reveals no blips, only a faint line indicating distant coastline to starboard. The radio sputters occasionally with static and the Coast Guard interrupts the silence with repeats of the urgent high wind warning. Gusts sing through the mast stays and my flashlight beam on the meter reveals that some of them exceed eighty knots. The compass light is off, and out the windows when the bow resurfaces from under the crest of a swell, ghostly white patches of foam break the blackness.

The captain is in the driver's seat, a black naugahyde swivel chair, his feet braced on the mahogany dashboard rail. I'm behind him, wedged into the uncomfortable, built-in bench space next to the chart table. For twenty-four hours, it has been impossible to stand without hanging on to something. We know of two other boats out here, a ninety-two-foot aluminum fish processor and a sixty-five-foot fish packer. They are both heading our way more than sixty miles ahead of us. The packer told the Coast Guard he'll try to get into the harbor at Yakutat. My captain says that since the packer has no tow, it's possible, but risky with this wind and the sea condition. The processor will keep coming, but we'll be miles apart when we pass.

The silence is broken with a static hiss. A man's voice comes on with a Mayday call. The transmission is remarkably clear, static free, coming through like the boat is nearby, as if the person talking is in the room with us.

The guy seems amazingly calm as he says they are taking on water in the stern and have launched the life raft. Six of the nine men are already in the raft. As he gives his position in latitude and longitude, we hear a crashing sound like dishes breaking. The radio mike stays keyed and the voice comes back saying they've rolled and the boat is now on its side.

The radio goes dead and the silence is palpable.

When the watch ends and I'm trying to sleep, knees and elbows pushing the bunk's plywood sideboard, back and butt against the steel of the wall, the motion of the boat changes. Currents from the north and south meet here and the long, huge but predictable swells are disrupted, making the sea sharp and confused. The alarm siren blares. This time, before I head below, I put on my coveralls and shoes. There won't be any sleeping for several hours.

The alarm panel is next to the workbench at the bottom of the ladder, and it's an effort to not be thrown off my feet. I thread my left arm through the railing. Between alarms, I take a little weight off my feet by hanging my butt on a ladder rung. Alarm lights I've never before had to deal with flicker just long enough to set off the siren. I decide to disconnect it. We're at the mercy of the hull, the machinery, and fate. All I can do is stay down here, hang on, watch for something serious, and do my best.

In the shipyard, when this boat is on dry dock, it looks huge, not like something that can be tossed about mercilessly. New tugs look like tadpoles under the water, deep and massive forward, shallow aft, leaving nothing to restrict water flow to the propellers. This hull is an old design. Under water, it's very graceful, beautiful actually, shaped like a canoe with a fantail extension above the rudder and a huge, five-bladed, stainless steel propeller. At one hundred and thirteen feet, it's slightly longer than the Mayflower, which was of similar tonnage (cubic feet of hull displacement, not actual weight). One hundred and two of the one hundred and thirty people on that voyage sailed to escape Europe, to start a new life. There are eight of us on this voyage. We're out here on our own in a storm presumably for the same reasons as the crew of the Mayflower, to earn a living.

In my mind, I visualize the whole boat as I know it, above and below the water line. I picture it from a distance through the darkness outside. Port and starboard running lights, red and green, three towing lights on the mast, yellow circles of light from fiddley and galley portholes. Insignificant flotsam on a vast ocean. Or, a gracefully constructed, ghostly, mechanical sea beast. The machine got us here. If we're to get out of this, it will be the machine that saves us. My robot elephant thunders beside me.

I think of my daughter and my wife at home, and pat the elephant's flank. I manage to circumnavigate the engine room, supporting myself by clinging to pipes, conduit, pumps and machinery. I see no leaks, no fires. The propeller shaft is turning. I return to my perch near the alarm panel and hang on for what seems like hours and hours.

Occasionally I venture up to the pilothouse and report. The passageways are all slippery wet. But we aren't sinking. When daylight finally comes, we can see Kayak Island on the radar. Its lee offers a place to hide. We shorten the towline and spend two gray days looking out over whitecaps in pelting rain, idling in circles. When we make radio contact with our company, we sense impatience with the delay. When the storm subsides, we cross the final stretch of open water. Inside Cape Hinchinbrook, we learn that the ship scheduled to unload after us arrived before us, and is occupying our berth. For another day-and-a-half, we idle in circles.

At the dock in Cordova, we moor the dry cargo barge carrying building supplies outside the container barge, and the boat outside of it. The longshoremen start to unload. The containers are locked together three deep over the whole barge, and it takes almost as long for them to remove the heavy chain lashings as it does for the crane operator to set the containers on the dock. By late afternoon they're done. Whatever is in the remaining containers, one row, three boxes high at each end of the barge, must be heavy.

The container barge is a rust bucket, two-thirds as big as a football field. It, like the boat and me, was leased just for this trip. The cleared expanse of the midsection seems bowed upward. I go to the corner, lie on the deck, and sight. I'm guessing at least four inches, maybe six, of arc. I pull the manhole covers in the exposed area. Inside the compartments, on the bottom of the hull thick sheets of rust appear in my flashlight beam. In just the small area I can see from each manhole, there's enough loose rust to fill several wheelbarrows, but no evidence of serious leaking.

For several months during the spring on the mudflats near the offices of the company leasing me and the boat for this trip, there were two halves of a broken steel barge. It was a rust bucket like this one, waiting for an insurance company ruling. This barge probably wouldn't have held together in our storm loaded only on the ends like it is now. If I pump water into the compartments amidships, it will take the arc out and remove the stress on the hull. I inform the captain.

I tell the deckhand from my watch I'll be okay alone if he wants to get off the boat, but I can use him if he wants the extra pay. Town wins. The pumping goes well. I sit in the sun on an upturned five-gallon bucket far enough away from the pumps so the noise isn't bad. Both barges and all the remaining cargo are now bound for Kenai. I'm working on the second can from the six-pack of cold beer sent from the crew, delivered by the cab driver.

This will be the last beer until the pumping is done. The barge is floating high enough that I can see across the dock. The taxi that brought the beer pulls up at the entry gate, and a guy with a full beard, wearing a red plaid shirt and Levi's, gets out. He looks like the picture on Brawny paper towel rolls. I assume he's a port guy until he focuses his attention on me and heads my way.

At the edge of the dock, close enough for me to hear over the pump motors, he yells, asking for the captain. I tell him that the crew went to town. I can see he's not too pleased and watch him zeroing in on my Rainier can and the empty one on the deck next to me. He introduces himself as one of the company's marine operations managers. I introduce myself back. I was part of the agreement when the boat was leased to his company, and he asks what I'm doing.

First I show him the rust in the two hull compartments that are still empty. Then I make him lie on the deck and sight the two-hundred-thirty feet to the other end so he can see what remains of the arc. He sees it and says it's probably normal for a barge loaded the way this one is, and that we are behind schedule and it's costing the company money. They had expected us to get underway as soon as the containers were off.

Without shutting my eyes, I'm still seeing the stern deck awash and hearing the chain shifting. Part of me is still hanging on at the base of the engine room ladder watching the alarm panel, or working my way around the engine room, hoping the World War II-vintage machinery and plumbing will hold together. The few days of idling in protected water with some chance for sleep haven't done much to make the visions fade.

I remind him of the broken barge on the mud flats near his office and bring up another one that sat on a rock-pile off of Vancouver Island for a winter.

He says, "They both broke in winter and this is summer."

I say, "Yeah, but you weren't out there. We were, along with three guys who didn't make it to the life raft and are still in their sunken fish processor. And after what we've been through, you're lucky the crew is willing to leave in the morning, but I'll be done with the ballasting by midnight. I'm sure you can find the captain in town and sort it out with him."

About the time I finish pumping, the watch deckhand shows up. The office guy is still drinking with the crew. He must have gotten an earful and calmed down. It isn't quite dark yet, so I walk the mile or so to town and find a place to mail a postcard from the stash I keep in my stateroom desk. I buy them in away ports and try to get pictures of eagles, whales, seals and bears, pictures that would be interesting to a little girl. I find the crew and have a beer or two before most of us cram into a cab back to the boat where I fall asleep without getting undressed.

In the morning we discover that the last guy to come back fell in when he tried to jump the gap between the two barges. The tide had changed, and current flowing away from the dock had pushed them apart. Fortunately, he didn't hit his head, and in the icy water, was able to work his way out from between, and across the barge stern to the dock. When he couldn't find a ladder, he pulled himself from piling to piling under the dock to a seiner on the other side. The seiner crew, still up drinking, heard his shouts and pulled him aboard. We let him stay in bed while we made up the tow.

The only memorable part of the rest of the trip was the view of Mount Redoubt from Cook Inlet where the currents, the deep draft of our boat and its lack of maneuverability from having a single-screw (propeller) made it unsafe for us to navigate the Kenai River. We idled for a few more gray days, waiting for our emptied barges to be brought back by the two small tugs that took them from us.

Most of the time, my life was full enough to suppress the black moods. Boat life gave me a way to grow that provided enough space for me to avoid the kind of setbacks that would have brought the depression to the forefront. My sister Kate's husband's suicide had forced me to consider the reality of the damage to other lives caused by giving in to the draw of that dark hole of depression. The pain his death caused didn't make my black moods go away, but it created a check that helped contain them.

Seventeen

My father and I had started connecting in a new way, and it felt like we were getting along better than ever. He seemed to need me, and I made time for him. He was confiding in me about his wife wanting to move, asking my advice and sometimes taking it. He had started showing me the respect I had been waiting my whole life for. The fact that he was confused about some things was inconsequential compared to his new directness with me, and I was starting to see little bits and pieces of the man behind what I had come to see as the mask that he had always presented.

I have told my brothers and sisters that I wished we could have a few beers with him, get him loosened up and talk about his life and ours. He has always loved to talk, to be the center of attention. He'll ramble on and on about old church people I never knew or have forgotten, or about how the guy who fixed his washing machine went to a church in California with the niece of someone he knew and went to church with back home, which he seems to take as proof that the man is a good Christian. The inference, if not the stated conclusion, is that the man has great skill and integrity and the washing machine would have cost twice as much to fix, and he would have been cheated if the man had been someone who wasn't connected to a church and born-again.

I have most of the pictures from his side of the family in my attic. Now, more than ever, he gets lost in that time before my mother and before the war. He is able to remember people and places from then with clarity, while he's trying to convince me that I'm not his son but someone else. I have his high school yearbooks and I have looked through them with him.

I had hoped that the pictures and yearbooks, along with the disease, would open the door and get him started and, for once, he would ramble on about something I want to hear, something that would help me understand him better and how he became who he was, what gave him that ferocious commitment to his God, and why he defined God the way he did. It didn't work that way. I had to fish and he seemed guarded. He answered some of my questions, but I learned only a few details that shed very little light.

He wasn't pictured or listed with any of the sports teams or clubs. I knew he worked at the newspaper after school and didn't have time for sports. When I was growing up, he told me that sports were frivolous and referred to athletes as spoiled meatheads who were glorified without cause. Playing football and wrestling were part of my rebellion. I don't remember him ever coming to watch me in any athletic event. As we looked through the pictures he told me that his older sister also worked at the newspaper. She got him the job and she had a car. She took him to school in the morning and brought him home after work at night. I didn't get much more about her than that.

He was fifteen in 1929 when the stock market crashed. Near that time his father came down with a debilitating disease that left him unable to do any of the hard, physical work required to run the farm. I think it was multiple sclerosis. I remember my grandfather as a skeletal old man whose arms jerked when he walked. He spent most of his time sitting in a rocker by the wood stove in the farmhouse parlor when we visited at Christmas, or in a wooden yard chair in the sun in the summer. He never spoke to me and I had no exchange with him at all. My father was the oldest boy still living at home when the trouble hit. There was a mortgage on the farm that, as he put it, his father had taken out to buy a car and hook up electric lights. Unnecessary luxuries. By default, it became my father's responsibility to pay off the loan and support the family until the younger children were grown.

That's the part of the story I had learned when, usually angry, he let me know how easy I had it. I knew about refinancing the mortgage through the government land bank for a lower interest rate, and paying off the bank. I knew about the crawler tractor he bought that enabled him to clear and plow land for other farmers at night after his own work was done, so he could pay off the mortgage quicker. And I knew about the hog farm he had a partnership in just before World War II broke out, and then the army stories that he told over and over as if that was the only time in his life he ever felt really alive, even though he was stationed in Seattle during the war and never left, except for schooling in California and Texas and for training in the desert in Eastern Washington.

I want to know what he was afraid of and why he thinks God is so angry. I want him to tell me about himself as you would a friend. I want to know what he did when he had a little free time, if he was angry with his dad like I was with him, what his love life before my mother—there has to have been one—was like. I want to know if he ever got drunk, got in a fight, or felt like killing himself. I want to know things people often don't find out about their dad, but wished they did. While we were looking at his old pictures I started asking him questions and watched the wall go up.

He starts talking about the Lord, and as usual it sounds canned, as though he's sealed off a whole side of himself and can only talk about what he thinks God would want him to say, not what really goes through his mind. So the picture trick didn't work, but since the night he let me hit him, I have sensed that behind the wall of Bible dogma that is now being replaced, or at least patched up with a slightly more penetrable one of confusion, there is something buried that I would like to know about.

Eighteen

On the days I take care of him, I try to schedule errands that take a lot of driving so I can accomplish something else that's useful too. He's easier to manage in the car. He can't move furniture around like he does at home or go running off down the street to some distant place from another time that he thinks is just across the field, even though we live in town and there are no fields nearby. In the car, we have a sense of mission, of purpose. We're on I-5 again, this time south of Everett heading north towards home. It's winter, late afternoon, and it's already getting dark. He's strapped in, and even when he disagrees with where we're going and gets agitated, he's stuck.

The box of old family pictures that we went to Seattle to get from my sister, Lilly, is in the trunk. They're from my mother's side of the family and my daughter needs them for a school assignment about her heritage. The last time I saw my mother before she died I shook her hand.

After two mastectomies, her breast cancer had metastasized. We both knew she was dying and we suspected it was the last time we would see each other. I had the impulse to hug her, and if I had the chance to do it again I would find a way to make that contact without hurting her fragile, pain-wracked body. But we shook hands because it would have been out of character to hug. It would have been an acknowledgement that we were at the end, which neither of us was ready to admit openly.

So we shook hands because our account was settled. She was telling me that I was up and running and she had faith in me. She had done her duty by me and I was launched. She was right, even though I couldn't see it yet, and I was telling her that I also believed she had done her duty and that I was grateful and at least beginning to appreciate how far it had stretched her.

Since acquiring the belief when I was a kid that I was doomed to hell, I hadn't cried at all about anything, even about the break-up of my marriage. I was cleaning the armature on the main generator when, to get my attention over the wood-planer scream of the tug's locomotive engine, the WWII submarine diving alarm sounded and the blue light flashed. We were outbound in the Straight of Juan de Fuca, approaching Dungeness Spit. There was a phone I was supposed to pick up in a booth that deadened the sound just enough to hear the voice from the pilothouse. I didn't go to it because I knew instantly what it was about. And to my absolute amazement, I wept uncontrollably, shamelessly and deeply. When I regained my composure, I climbed to the pilothouse and stood in the dark as the lighthouse went by and the captain told me what I already knew. They dropped me off at the pulp mill dock in Port Angeles where my relief was waiting.

Before she died, while she was sick, I had the chance to talk openly with my mother about growing up, about her religion and about my life. She tried to bridge the religion gap and we seemed to connect. She told me about my father's reaction when he found out my sister, Lilly, was pregnant and that the baby's father was black, about how he loaded a gun and she stopped him at the door. I wanted the same openness from my father, but his world and my world seemed to exist in different dimensions.

I'm sure he appeared different to probably everyone else that knew him than he did to us, his kids. It seemed to me that his vision of God had narrowed his view of the world, and with those that shared his vision, he was free to be open and warm. He had a good side. He could be, and was, very warm to people outside his faith if they were innocent, which meant they had to be potential converts who had not come over because they didn't know any better, hadn't been reached yet. Part of reaching them was being kind, generous and understanding.

He was kind when there was nothing in the way to impede it, but with us there were complications. We were born into his faith. We had seen it up close and had no excuse not to accept it. In our individual ways, we all said no to his particular version of God. And we did it separately. We were not soul mates who bonded for protection. There definitely was a shared experience, but we didn't know we were bonded by it until we were grown. We didn't fight among ourselves any more than most kids, and we did spend some time with each other, but each of us found his or her own track and followed it. It wasn't until we were grown and our mother had died that we learned how tied together we really are.

I find myself suspecting that he's hiding in there behind all that confusion, and may have more control than he lets on. Mostly, though, he demands attention with what seems on the surface to be nonsense.

"I was in a parade," he says.

"Oh. How did that come about?" I say.

"The last time I came through here, and you may not know it, but I'm quite a celebrity."

"The parade was for you then?"

"There were two of us," he says. "She was with me and we worked together on it. It was quite a deal. It helped end the war."

"So what did you do? Maybe I've read about it."

He's telling me an old story again. It's an Alzheimer's story that he repeats often. It's about his stay in the hospital. Providence Hospital is just west of where we are on the freeway now, over the hill with a view of Port Gardner Bay. The story is a little different each time, but it has the same theme. And he's the hero. Sometimes he includes his wife because she was there too, though he usually can't name her and her role in it changes, but I know whom he's talking about. This time they're both heroes. It always happened during the war, which, in his mind, was very recent, and they were involved in research.

"You know, the gasket material they use in the engine, like the engine in this car. It keeps the oil and the carbon from mixing with the fire and the water."

"What about it?" I ask.

"We helped them develop it."

"How did you do that?"

"The stuff was awful and I had to drink gallons of it; then they put me in a machine and checked to see if it would leak out and it did. So they kept experimenting around until they found the right stuff. They said they couldn't have done it without me."

"You must be pretty proud of yourself," I say.

He had had colon surgery and had to drink the barium tracer they use when they X-ray your intestinal tract. He's right. It's awful.

"There was quite a lot of intrigue around it," he says.

"I remember that," I say. "You kicked some poor lady who was just trying to do her job and take a blood sample."

"That's what they tell me," he says. "There were awful things going on in that place, perverted things. They had me down in the basement. They were homosexuals, and I don't know what they had planned for me, but I told the Lord that I wouldn't dishonor him, and they were bringing my little girl in."

"So you kicked the nurse and sent her tray of vials flying and they broke, and she couldn't take your blood, so you had to stay in the hospital an extra day."

"I would've done more than that."

"I know. You tried to throw your IV unit through the fourth-floor window."

"I'm not afraid to stand up and be counted."

"No one was counting you, Dad. They were trying to help you, and you were making it hard. You were never in the basement. You never left your hospital room, and one of us was with you nearly all of the time."

"That's what they tell me," he says.

The actual surgery happened later in a separate hospital stay that lasted for a week. The time we're talking about was to have been an overnighter, a short visit mainly to confirm their diagnosis, but they had to look up his rectum with a scope and it made a big impression on him. He made trouble and it took them three days to learn what they wanted to know. One of us was with him for much of it. The reason he was alone just before the incident was that we were all at a family-support meeting with the psychiatrist a few blocks away and we didn't know yet about the hallucinations he would have or the dramatic turn for the worse he would take—a change that would mean none of us could deny any longer that something serious was happening.

His wife knew he was slipping first. I didn't want to believe there was any more wrong with him than could be explained simply by the fact that he was getting old. None of us, my brothers and sisters and I, wanted to believe her because we knew she was unhappy about other things in their life and we thought she was just supporting her argument. She started taking him to doctors anyway, and I started spending more time with him, and by the time he went in the hospital I was convinced.

I had taken him to an appointment with a geriatric psychiatrist where he took a test that was supposed to reveal whether or not he suffered from dementia, and if so, the extent of it. He wanted me to go with him. I was the mediator, the impartial witness who would help him convince her that nothing was wrong, at least not wrong enough to support her argument to leave the farm and move to town, and not even the town down the hill, which would still be near my brothers, but the one her son lived in ten miles away. He definitely did not want to go and she was miserable and could think of nothing else.

It surprised me that she couldn't see and didn't know that if you were to have my father, you had to take the farm too. I couldn't imagine him anywhere but on his farm. I had always assumed that he would fade away reading his Bible in his recliner in front of his fireplace, or drop dead cutting firewood or plowing. Moving was a completely alien idea, and I was sure he would whither and die in a short time in the kind of house, living the kind of life, she wanted and needed in town.

The old cabin and barn, the trees, the rocky fields, the dog, the tractor and the pick-up were part of what he needed to live, and the place had become part of him and he had become part of it. It was his farm and the house was incidental to it. She probably thought of the house on the farm as my mother's. My mother had paid for it and lived there with him because the word divorce wasn't in her vocabulary, and she knew it was her only chance at happiness until she realized that happiness was beyond her grasp and got cancer and died.

There was no happy solution to this situation either. He was between a rock and a hard place, with nowhere to go. His wife had tried living his way, on the farm, and it had become clear to her, even with what concessions he was willing to make, that it wasn't where she wanted to spend the rest of her life. He couldn't face life without her and was starting to at least entertain the thought of moving, though it was clear he didn't like it.

I drove him in my car to the appointment because I had already made him give me his driver's license. A trip to the dump with him in his pick-up had convinced me that he was dangerous, not only to himself but to some poor innocent family like mine that might happen to be in the wrong place at the wrong time. I saw his driving as something that happened to a lot of old people. In his own element he still seemed pretty normal. I had trouble keeping up with him on the farm, cutting and splitting wood or bucking the hay bales he bought to supplement the hay he grew. Town, with a good hospital and fire department, was just down the hill and my two brothers lived close-by and were available to help, so I supported his desire to stay on the farm.

The test didn't change my opinion about their moving, but it clarified that he had a problem. He knew what year he was born, but he didn't know what month it was now, what day or year it was, when his birthday was, who was president, and he couldn't follow simple instructions or carry out simple finger exercises. He had already seen a battery of medical doctors and eliminated most of the possible causes, and after the psychiatric test, they came up with an official diagnosis. They said he had dementia of the Alzheimer's type. At the time, they couldn't actually confirm Alzheimer's disease until the patient was dead and they could take a sample of brain tissue. It was in the early stages, so we were hopeful. Instead of his wife, he made me his legal guardian and gave me power of attorney.

He was also anemic. They suspected it was caused by a ruptured blood vessel in his colon that bled continually. They reasoned that the anemia from the blood loss caused the fatigue that contributed to his confusion. They said it was repairable and it gave us hope for some improvement, so into the hospital he went.

He said he was trying to protect Lilly, my sister, from some vague intrigue or conspiracy that involved sex. She was coming into the room, stopping for a visit on her way home from the meeting with the psychiatrist. His wife had been at the meeting too, but hadn't lingered to talk to me outside like my sister had, so she got there first and was in the room already along with the nurse. The woman with the tray came in ahead of my sister and before they were able to calm him, he had kicked the tray and tried to throw the I.V. unit through the window.

There was hope that the hallucinations were from the medication and that when the anemia was corrected some of the confusion would go away. When he went back in the hospital for colon surgery, his wife stayed with him in the room, taking her meals there and sleeping in a bed they brought for her. He was there for a week, on the same floor with the same nurses as before, and the hospital was grateful to have her, as I was.

At first, my brothers and sisters and I took turns giving her a break so she could get away, and I suppose she was grateful to have us. He was old and sick and we would do what needed to be done. We had all been wounded by him and had wounded him back, but we were all there to take our turn when it was necessary to have someone with him who was familiar, to calm him and keep him from hurting himself or someone else. I was feeling pretty good about the way my family was pulling together.

When my sister, Kate, told us she couldn't be in the same room with him anymore, it only made a slight ripple. We adjusted and took turns covering the time she would have been at the hospital. Her story came out bit by bit over time, but that hospital stay changed my father irrevocably.

After he got out of the hospital, his wife continued to care for him. He soon became too much for her, and there was the call at night. She couldn't handle it anymore. He had left the house and was out in the woods somewhere. The group home we tried to put him in couldn't handle him either. And though it wasn't like she envisioned, his wife's wish came true. She got to move to the town where her son lived. We took over my father's care.

There's a steady pelting rain now. In the dark, the glare of headlights on the wet windshield and windows makes it a little hard to see but, though traffic is heavy, it's flowing and I don't mind the drive.

"Hadn't we better pull over?" he says.

"Why?" I ask.

"I'm getting too old for this."

"You mean riding in the car?"

I look at him and he's worried, almost scared. It's warm enough and comfortable inside the car. We're traveling the speed limit, moving with the traffic, and his eyes are darting from the rearview mirror to the windows, from the taillights ahead to the oncoming headlights in the southbound lanes across the divider.

"Shall we pull over? I never was very good at this racing business," he says.

"We're just going home," I say. "What would we do if we pulled over?"

"Let 'em all go by," he says. "Get out of the race and let someone else win. I'm too old for this."

"They'll just keep coming," I say, "and we would be late for dinner."

I keep driving but I can see that he's still tense, so I explain rush hour to him and ask him to hang on and tell him that we'll be home soon. He's quiet, but the look doesn't go away and I feel guilty all the way home.

At dinner, I'm not sitting next to him so it shouldn't be getting to me, but it is. It's like getting seasick. By the time you realize it's coming on and decide to find a porthole or go out on deck for some air, it's too late. He's finally quit talking and started eating. My wife still listens to him and tries to respond as if he's making sense. She's that way; she'd make a good nurse. He's transformed her agreeableness into the belief that she's born-again. It allows him to like her and it makes her an ally.

He's been rattling off stories about how the Lord has a hand in even the most insignificant details of his life. What anyone else would see as coincidence, usually a very minor coincidence, he attributes to the guiding hand of the Lord. Everything in his life has to have a connection with the Lord. "His eye is on the sparrow. . . " He has that glassy, beaming look on his face. When something is sanctioned by the Lord, you'd better not question it. I let him talk, trying to be polite without listening.

He's eating mashed potatoes and gravy. We made them especially for him because I know he likes them with pot roast. We never have mashed potatoes. He's smacking his lips like a dog trying to eat soft, canned food. It's loud. He's always chewed loudly, but this is without any restraint. When I was a kid, the closer he was to popping, the louder the smacking got, and judging from the noise now, I'm about due for a backhand across the face that will send me and my chair into the next room.

I look across the table at my kids. They're both eating quietly. They're always polite to Grandpa. He hasn't spent a lot of time with them, so it's a little formal. They know he's sick and they do their best. My daughter is about the same age I was when the backhands were often part of what was for dinner. The smacking seems to get louder. I watch him eat for a moment, then excuse myself, saying I have to go to the bathroom.

In the bathroom I don't know what to do. I don't have to go. I usually didn't back when I was young either. I stand in front of the mirror now and remember the hate-poisoned face that used to look back at me. It gives me a chill. The face in the mirror now is a lot different, and it's not thinking about a gun. My face looks a little stressed, but pretty sane.

I put down the toilet seat lid and sit on it. I do a meditation exercise and listen to the quiet. He's just a sick old man and I'm the adult now. Those are my kids out there, and my wife, and the twisted face in the mirror is gone and the gun in this room is his old shotgun, disassembled and benign, wrapped and hidden, by me, behind the hot water tank, not the snub-nosed thirty-eight that was in a shaving kit on top of the linen closet in our house when I was my daughter's age.

I think my kids are still my friends. They're just kids, my kids, and I miss them when my work takes me away from home. I think they're good kids, and sometimes I worry that they won't develop character because their life isn't crazy enough. But each of us gets his or her own life equation to solve, and they all seem to stretch us to our limits.

So I'm sitting on the toilet doing relaxation breathing because my father is a noisy eater and it makes me remember being a kid at his table. I've been in the bathroom a long time and I know I should get back to him. You can't tell what he'll do next and I should be there, just in case. I flush the toilet, wash my hands and go back to the dining room. They're finishing up and no one seems troubled that I was gone.

Nineteen

"I don't know about this!" he says.

The road winds up the hill from town and we're almost to the farm. My seven-year-old son is sitting between us in the cab.

"What do you mean?" I say.

"It just doesn't seem right."

"What?"

"All this."

"All what?"

"You know. This project that we're getting involved in."

"You mean making hay at your house. We've been doing it for years. We'll have more help than usual. We'll have pizza and Pepsi for lunch. What could be wrong with that? You'll get to see your grandkids."

"I don't know," he says. "I just don't like it."

He doesn't say anything more. I'm wary, but not concerned yet. I'm hoping to get him focused on the work. If he feels productive doing something he knows how to do, time passes more easily.

We've been making hay since we got our first pet goat when I was eight or nine. I remember surprising field mice as we raked the hay with pitchforks and made shocks. We had helped him frame a barn with poles made from trees cleared at the house site. We sided it with rough lumber milled from the bigger logs. The pet goat became goats, which were joined by a pony. When I was ten, they let me buy the horse with paper route money. Then there were more horses. We hauled the hay home un-baled, loose, on one of the flatbed trucks owned by Gethsemane. Back then, even on public roads, we kids could ride on top of the load. We used a converted horse-drawn mower pulled by a small, primitive tractor to cut the hay. Turning someone's unused pasture grass into hay is as much a part of my memories as my sense of helplessness, his disappointment in me, and his anger.

My attachment to Scout had sealed my investment in the hot, dusty work of stowing loose hay in that barn, and the sense of obligation stayed with me, so every year since that I could break free, I've helped. We no longer need the hay. It's curious how the last two horses died within a few months of each other, as if they sensed it was their time, and avoided being another complication of my father's disease. The few steers my youngest brother is keeping on the place will be butchered in the fall.

The weather is cooperating and we have a good turnout. My brother, Daniel, is already here with his two boys and my dad's dog when we pull up. David, my youngest brother, who bought land from my father, comes out of the house he built here. We park in front of the old cabin, under the chestnut tree still standing in what now is David's front yard. The dog runs up, tail wagging, and fawns over Dad as he gets out of the truck. He's clearly glad to see her and seems to recognize everyone else, if not by name at least as people who are friendly. For a short while, he seems content.

Kate's son, now in college, has joined us, and my older sister, Lilly, comes with her son. There's still enough loose hay in the barn from last year for the kids to swing from the rope and jump while we get organized. With all the help, and because this time David and I paid a neighbor to make bales, the job should be easy. The tradition gets an extension.

His place is a patchwork of small three-to-five-acre fields carved out of alder and evergreen woods. The fields are bumpy and some of them are a long way from the barn. We've taken the sideboards off of my small flatbed truck to make loading easier, and there are enough of us so that it's efficient to keep a driver in the truck, stopping for the closest bales to be loaded and stacked. We rotate jobs, lifting the bales onto the truck, receiving and interweaving them on the bed so they don't bounce off, and driving.

The field we start on is near the back of his property. When he tries to drag a bale, the twine breaks and it falls apart. He can't lift one onto the bed. When I try to help, he gets angry and starts pulling bales off the truck. I tell him he's the foreman here and doesn't have to work. He doesn't buy it. The younger grandkids know enough to stay out of the way, on top of the stack, so we try getting him to ride with them. He doesn't like the way my nephew and brother are assembling the load, gets angry again, and tries to jump off while the truck is moving.

When the first load is finally up, he doesn't protest as I guide him to the truck cab. The younger kids will ride back to the barn on top of the bales and the adults will walk. When my father realizes we're just going to the barn, his look changes. His hand goes to the door handle, and he's poised for a quick getaway as we bounce across the uneven stubble.

"I shouldn't be here," he says. "This is all wrong."

"You're making hay with your family," I say, "like we've done every year. How can that be wrong?"

He cuts his eyes at me. The look says I'm a liar.

He opens the door and when he jumps, I hit the brakes hard to keep from running him over. The kids on the load yell as a few unstable bales fall off. No one is hurt. We reload the spilled bales and I talk him back into the cab. I'm stressing. He's calling me by his older brother's name and still seems to trust that I'm on his side, so I have hope. He lets me buckle the seat belt, which I'm counting on to at least slow him if he tries to jump again.

Back at the barn, he gets out and paces. When he heads across the field, my sister brings him back and tries to occupy him while we unload. I belt him in the cab for another round. I'm miserable. He has that dinner-table, loud-chewing look that came before the backhand.

"I don't like this," he says.

"What don't you like?"

He responds with the sneer that says, *I'm on to you, and you know exactly what I'm talking about.* All I can do is keep repeating that we're just making hay, and he should be happy that his family wants to spend the day with him. It's not working. I'm desperate and relieved when we reach the field and Daniel agrees to take a turn.

So my little brother's in the cab with the old man, and I'm following the truck. I pass bales up to my grown nephew, and the work helps release my frustration. On top of the load, my son and his cousins are oblivious to the struggle that I imagine is still going on in the cab. They're having the hay-day experience, making a memory.

Before he got sick, my father and I had come to understand that our respective refusal to give in to the other was based in a form of love. When he made me his legal guardian, the validation it represented was huge, but so is the responsibility. When it was clear my father needed full-time care to keep from being committed to the Alzheimer's ward, I could not have done it. Daniel volunteered and took leave from his job. I feel bad because it's his day off.

Daniel is two years younger than I am. His way of being true to himself isn't as confrontational as mine. He rebelled later than I did, and in a different way. When he was twenty, my father thought he was crazy and wanted my help in having him forcibly committed to an institution. I refused because I believed Daniel was doing what I had done, finding and validating his own truth. It was no small task and it was bound to be messy. He was expressing legitimate reactions to what I saw as my father's warped reality.

Back at the barn, Daniel positions the truck for unloading and gets out. He stands back and watches us unload. *My dad stays in the cab!* I climb down. He's leaning forward with his face close to the windshield, holding the heater knobs on the dashboard. He seems to be concentrating intently. My brother is talking to one of his boys. I cut in.

"All right, what did you do?"

There's a faint smile.

"Why isn't he out here accusing us of something?" I persist.

"He's busy. He's got a job to do."

"So, what's he doing?"

"He's waiting."

"For what?"

"The right moment."

"The right moment to do what?"

"To drop the bombs."

"Bombs?"

My brother can see that I'm starting to get it. He says,

"It's too much work to fight him, and you can't win. You never could. He's as stubborn as ever, and what rationality he had is gone, so I try to find out where he is and go there with him."

"What did you say to him? I couldn't even get him to tell me what was wrong."

"He doesn't want to be here, so I asked him where he wanted to go. He started rambling about the war like he always does. So I helped him build a story and gave him a job that he thinks is important. I let him be right, then put him in control and make him tell me what he wants to do. Then I try to guide it. We're bombing. I don't know what we're bombing. But he seems to, and it's helping him fix whatever it is he's upset about. I got lucky. It's working this time. Sometimes it backfires and makes the situation worse."

When it's time to go back to the field, my brother gets in the truck.

"Okay, Beryl, let 'em go," he says.

My father pulls out the heater knob that directs heat from the blower to defrost the windshield. The blower is off.

"I'll bet that got 'em," Daniel says. "Good work."

The rest of the day passes pleasantly. The bombardier stays in the cab, and my brother continues driving the truck. Somehow the transition to the yard for pizza and Pepsi is made. After eating, we finish the job and leave, tired.

At the Ascension Ministries nursing home on the day we admit him, Lilly takes a picture of Dad, Daniel, and me with the administration building in the background. The same poplar trees line the Av as when we were kids. Kate and David are not with us.

The nursing home people are nice. He will be well cared for. In the business meeting, while we're listening to the spiel and I'm signing the papers, the woman uses my name three times instead of Dad's in reference to him. She calls the pharmacy and tells them that Bill Smith is a new resident, then she says it to a nurse's station, and once again in reference to the paperwork we're signing. As his legal guardian, my name is on the paperwork along with his. I say, joking but only sort of, that if she does it again I'll jump through the window and escape.

When we leave, Daniel says, "They've got him back."

I say, "We had our eighteen months."

Daniel says, "He always belonged to them more than us anyway."

Twenty

A few days after we put him in the nursing home, I go in for a physical. I haven't had one for several years. I'm feeling run down, exhausted, but the feeling seems reasonable. Besides being stressed by my father's situation, I've been working hard. I'm still working on tugboats, now as mate. We mostly move wood products from ports in Canada to west coast American ports, usually Seattle, but sometimes Portland, San Francisco or Los Angeles. In Puget Sound ports, the crew also acts as longshoremen, driving forklifts. The pay is good but there isn't much time for sleep. I've been working on boats for twenty years and the novelty has worn off. By moving from the engine room to the pilothouse, I'm trying to make a career change of sorts, but I'm tired of the life. Though my wife is doing a good job of covering for me when I'm absent, there are better ways to be a good father.

The first set of blood tests sets off alarms that result in a barrage of tests, including a bone marrow biopsy. Blood is made in the marrow. It's the factory and it's supposed to produce several kinds of cells. Each of them does a specific job to keep the body running right. Sometimes the programming goes bad, quality control goes out the window and the wrong stuff gets made. A biopsy isn't much different from a blood draw, except that it's more invasive; it goes straight to the source in the center of the bone, and it is more painful.

I'm lying face down on an examining table with my pants and underwear pushed down to expose the upper part of my butt, not a very dignified position. The marrow is drawn from the pelvic bone. On both sides at the very bottom of the back, there's a place where the pelvis is close to the surface. They're going to drill there. The tool they use looks like and is about the same size as a simple T-shaped corkscrew, except the screw part looks more like a long, very thick needle cut to a sharp bevel at the end. The needle is made of two pieces, a hollow casing tube with a solid shaft filling the center. The shaft is designed to be pulled out once the point has been forced through the hard outer bone into the soft core, drawing the marrow sample into the tube.

To distract from the pain, I bite hard on the corner of the pillow. It really hurts! I think the procedure is new to the doctor taking the sample.

Since my case is an unusual puzzle, several doctors and nurses have been summoned to the room. They're calling what they draw a dry tap. No blood, just white stuff. Out of disbelief because the sample looks so wrong, they drill me again in my other hip. When the second draw gets the same result, I sense it's serious, but refuse to let the doom in the air sink in. It feels unreal, and I distance myself like I do when my father describes his Alzheimer's hallucinations about giant pigs with fangs in the yard, or a car driving down the neighbor's roof, as though they're real experiences.

Afterward, in her guarded way, the doctor tries to get my attention, but I let myself stay in denial, because it's convenient and all I can handle at the moment. It will take a few days for a lab to analyze the marrow sample. They send me home. Because no one has specifically said not to, I go to work on the tugboat and make a six-day trip to Gold River, British Columbia for a barge-load of newsprint and lumber. From a pay phone there, near the longshoremen's lunchroom, I call and learn that they want me to come in immediately. I say I will when we dock in Seattle, day after tomorrow.

While I'm on the boat, probably because I've started paying

attention, I notice changes in my body. I feel exhausted. I have sharp headaches. My color is bad and there are bruises where I have no memory of being bumped. Some old scars have developed into water blisters and others have turned red and become inflamed. A lump on my arm that started out looking like a pimple has grown into a knot the size of a walnut. I meditate every chance I get.

On the long drive from the dock in Seattle to my doctor's office in Anacortes, I prepare myself for the worst. This time there's no mincing. I'm told I'm seriously ill. If I have things I need to say to important people in my life, now's the time. There's some hope, but it's clear to me that I shouldn't count on it. They're uncertain what the disease is, but know it's a lymphoma and *not* in the early stages. I can see the not-altogether-successful struggle to be impassive in my doctor's face and hear the ring of truth in the words "very sick," but not much more. He's merely confirming reality.

I hear the ringing on the other end of the phone before it's picked up. I realize I'm going to have to say it out loud and that I don't want to believe it. I blurt it out.

"I won't be able to sail tonight."

"Why not? Are you okay?"

"I have cancer."

Long silence.

"What kind?"

"They're not sure yet. It's some kind of lymphoma."

Long silence.

"So you won't be coming back for a while?"

"I guess not."

"I'm sorry." Pause. "They're doing amazing things with cancer now. We'll just believe you're going to be all right. Don't worry about anything down here. Just do what you have to do to get well, and let us know as you know more."

"Thanks. I left my stuff on the boat. I'll try to get someone to come get it next time the boat's in town."

By saying it aloud, it has become much more real. The hospital receptionist's desk where I sit to call has a fake walnut top. Its image becomes seared in my memory.

The truly hard part is yet to come. Allie is still at work and won't be home for a few hours. I had gone straight from the boat to the doctor without checking in with her. At home, I get out of my old truck and stand in the driveway, staring at the dust on the red-painted steel of its door. I wipe my finger across the cool smoothness, then rub my finger and thumb together to savor the grittiness, the truth of dirt.

The idea of going into the house seems overwhelming. I take my bicycle from the garage and ride the short distance to the edge of town, then out through the farms toward the river. It's February, cool but not raining, and there's little wind. Clouds hide the snowy cone of Mt. Baker. The flatness of the muddy fields is broken by occasional farmhouses, sometimes in clusters for extended family, sometimes with nearby migrant shacks, and always surrounded by barns, outbuildings, poplar trees, and fruit trees.

I turn south along the road that runs parallel to the low evergreen-covered ridge that rises above and snakes across the bottomland then bends like a giant J, forcing the river to flow around its far side. The ridge rises from the flat, like the island it may once have been in the salt marsh that was here before the bottomland was diked and turned into farms. I stop and watch a red-tailed hawk fly away from its perch on a wire above me. I think about absence. I've been ignoring a cold feeling in my spine for months. My bone marrow is now producing dysfunctional mutant white cells and nothing else. My body, like my mother's body had done, is committing suicide.

When I was in my mid-twenties, I was diagnosed with high blood pressure. As part of his search for the cause, my doctor quizzed me about stress in my life and asked questions about depression. I'd never had to explain it the way you would to a doctor, as a symptom. Black moods, sadness and thoughts of suicide were familiar enough. I explained that the sense of hopelessness I've experienced and the accompanying sadness felt like logical responses to events in my life. The doctor didn't prescribe drugs, but sent me to a stress therapist. I learned to meditate. It's already helping me through this.

The black moods started when I was a kid questioning my parents' beliefs. The idea of checking out was a safety valve, a place to go when all the other doors seem closed. Thoughts of ending it were tempered by the notion that it was an unforgivable sin and would land me in hell. I didn't know I wasn't alone. I hadn't read *Hamlet* yet, or learned that a famous French guy named Albert Camus thought that the only real philosophical question is whether or not to commit suicide. Hopelessness inspired a kind of fearlessness that was really desperation. As the song says, "When you've got nothing, you've got nothing to lose."

Life has been a flirtation with oblivion, testing whether it was worth the effort. I looked for ways to be happy. If I failed, so what? I was already at rock bottom. Gradually I invested in hope, gaining confidence, but always hanging on to the familiar sadness of that safe, dark place.

Now I've built a world in baby steps, a day at a time, because it has felt right. I'm a dad. My absence will hurt people I care about. I've been distancing myself from the dark place, but something bigger than me is stepping in, saying Time's up.

Across the ridge, at the river, I leave the road for the dike, ignoring the private property signs. The river is high but not threatening flood, and I watch the water flow toward the shallow mudflats of the bay. I think about the mountain, the rain and snow, the waterfalls, the streams running through the woods converging, contributing, uniting in this motion, this power, this life, then dissipating and becoming lost in the immensity of Puget Sound and the Pacific Ocean. Mesmerized by the quiet gray-green motion of the moving mass, I let its life settle like a tiny warm seed in the pit of my stomach, momentarily distracting me from the hypothermic chill that has been quietly growing in my marrow.

Watching the river flow, watching its simple truth, is one of the few ways I understand the idea of prayer. The clouds are reflected on the surface of the rippled, moving water. As I smell the dirt of the surrounding farmland mixed with the cool, salt air, an involuntary feeling forms, a momentary feeling of wellbeing.

Across the river, the bank is lined with alder trees, their branches leafless, skeletal, exposing the lane that runs through them where it cuts close to the riverbank. I picture the campsites used by migrant families in the summer and steelhead fishermen in winter. I want at least one more summer with our daughter, our son, and Allie.

Back home, I still can't go into the house. I sit on the edge of the carport's concrete slab, my legs stretched over the crushed rock of the adjacent parking spot. Winter weeds have taken over the mud of our garden plot. I hear the distinctive, diesel sound of Allie's car as it rounds the corner and comes toward me. She parks and gets out.

We've been married over twenty years. We know each other well. She's lived with my bouts of depression, heard my stories about growing up. Our life together is not always graceful, but we've built a real family and know we're partners. She's my best friend and I don't know how to say it. I stand up and meet her eyes.

"I have cancer."

She's been trying to prepare herself.

"What kind?"

"Some kind of lymphoma. They think it's non-Hodgkin's,

whatever that means."

She buries her head on my chest and pounds on my shoulders.

"No, no, no, no."

"I'm sorry," I say.

We stand like that for what seems like a long time, then she pulls away and gets something out of the car. Her face is stricken and she's pulled deep inside herself.

"What else did they say?" she says.

"That I'm very sick."

"What are your chances?"

"They said some lymphomas are treatable. That probably means I'll be bald and radiated. They don't know yet. I have an appointment with a cancer doctor tomorrow morning."

I want her to hold me and feel sorry for me and make a fuss that will somehow fix it, but it doesn't happen. She's been holding this likelihood at a distance, waiting for a conclusive answer, and now that she has the wrong one, she's reeling.

"What are we going to tell the kids?"

"That I'm sick, but we don't know how sick, and that I'm going to go to a new doctor tomorrow to find out more. Then we'll take it a day or a week at a time and do the best we can."

"Don't you die on me!"

Twenty-one

I step through the open doorway into fluorescent brightness, organized clutter, and the intimacy of the small room. The woman at the computer terminal smiles as though she's glad I'm here. She's blonde, in her thirties, a little plump and wearing no make-up. I imagine her mothering small, well-behaved children when she's at home. If I've seen her before, I don't remember.

"I need to give you some blood," I say.

She motions to the familiar seat, beige plastic supported by chrome tubing. Once I'm sitting, the board-like armrest folds down and traps me like a child in a high chair. I lay out my right arm, exposing the pale blue of the vein that runs up the inner elbow. The arm is no longer tracked and bruised, and the vein is well hidden. She questions me with her eyes. She wants the slip from the doctor.

"Oncology." I give my name and cut my eyes toward the worn cardboard accordion file folder on a shelf above her computer. She studies me for a split second. She takes down the folder and finds my order. She's quiet as she selects the correct syringe and vials and says only the minimum as she feels for the vein, finds it and slides the needle in. She's good: the needle pricks but doesn't hurt.

There's something strangely enticing about the feeling of the needle in my arm, an association with intense emotion, combined fear and anticipation of hopeful news. It nearly always induces the same vision in my mind, something I witnessed long ago, and the image momentarily reappears as the needle pierces my

flesh. It was in the Sixties and I was eighteen. A high school friend
who had gone hippie was living in an old house on Capitol Hill
in Seattle.

I didn't know the girl and never saw her before or after. She
was an acquaintance of my friend, about my age, maybe younger.
She was shooting heroin; I was invited to watch. She was skinny
and looked unhealthy. Her mousy hair was unwashed, oily, and
her color was bad, as mine has become. When I entered the room,
she barely glanced up. She was focused and intent on the ritual with the powder in the teaspoon, the few drops of water, the
candle flame, the syringe and tourniquet. She found the vein and
winced as she forced the needle in. She depressed the plunger,
slowly pushing the liquid from the syringe into her bloodstream.
In a single wave her body relaxed and her eyes glazed with serenity. It was like watching an orgasm. Someone else took the
needle out.

It's that wave of serenity that comes up in my mind when
a needle goes in. I envy it, long for it, and it doesn't happen.
They're not putting potentially lethal happiness in; they're taking
blood out, reading a gauge like taking an oil sample from a mal-
functioning engine. They're looking for evidence of mutant cells,
contaminants that are destroying the machine from the inside.
Blood draws are the physical events that punctuate my life. The
needle goes in. The blood comes out. The seers read the signs and
tell me my future, and my need to know is almost stronger than
my hope or fear.

We watch my blood pulse into the glass tubes.

After she removes the needle, she puts a cotton ball over the
puncture to absorb the leakage. I press down on it while she gets
a piece of tape to hold it in place. I can feel her concern, and sense
that she would say something comforting if she knew the right
words.

"Wish me luck," I say as I stand to leave.

She gives me a grim smile. " We're not too busy right now, so the results should print out at the clinic within the hour. You take care."

The blood-draw ritual is over. It carries the anticipation of laying the cards face up on the table. The dealing is done. The composition and chemistry of my blood are no different now than they were before the needle. If my bone marrow is again producing mutant cells, not knowing won't negate the fact. And knowing won't do much to fix it. We're playing our best cards and if they're not good enough, the next stage is finding a way to deal with the results, deciding how to use what remaining time there is.

The suspense seems almost more excruciating than facing reality. It's exhausting and enticing. It would be easy to let go, give up, to slide into that familiar dark place I've known all my life. But, it would be so wrong now. I have kids, people who love me, reasons to hope. And though Hope came out of Pandora's box last, and with a broken wing, it doesn't die easily.

Not long ago, people waited weeks for results of similar tests. I live close to a hospital with a good lab. The doctors and nurses at the oncology clinic are like personal trainers, coaching me through this, the real struggle that every test and competition in my life has been a dry run for. They give me the details, let me read the same medical journal articles they read. They talk straight, whether the news is good or bad, and try to find a way to help me deal with it. An hour's wait isn't bad. But it's still a long hour.

My fate, my sentence, is no different from the lab lady's or the doctor's, or yours. No one gets out of life alive. We push the immediacy away to some other day, next year, next week, tomorrow, when we're old. We want to deny it or control it. So here I am with an hour to kill, waiting for numbers that will help me decide what to do with my immediate life, my remaining time. The like-

lihood of looming finality heightens the intensity. Two weeks ago
my blood counts were still very low, my immune system almost
nonexistent. If I catch a cold or eat some bad tuna, I'll probably
die from it. Today's odds are less than even in my favor. They
shot the silver bullet and it should have worked by now.

I'm not alone in the waiting area. There are three of us in the
half dozen chairs here at the end of a long hallway. The printer
where the blood test results will arrive is close by. I'm listening
for it to come alive with the dot matrix buzz that will reveal one
of our fates. Our end of the hall is lined on one side with three
examining rooms that have paper-thin walls. We're sitting in a
dead end beyond the door from the main corridor of this wing.
The area has been made cozy with nicely upholstered chairs and
lamps that shed soft light. Because of what happens here, it has a
more intimate feel than the cramped, make-do waiting room it is.

At the opposite end of the clinic there's a treatment room set
up like a living room, with recliners around a TV. Two hospital
beds near the far wall can be screened off by curtains. Outpatients
come here for chemo treatments. Some of them watch TV while
the chemicals drip into their blood. I've had my bone marrow
drawn on one of those beds. My chemo was experimental and
done in the hospital.

I am acutely aware of the other two patients waiting with me.
We acknowledge each other, but don't speak. They're not together, though they're close in age. He's chemo-bald under his baseball hat. His face has that hollow grey, jaundiced look, but his
dark eyes are alive and pleasant. They're both younger than I am,
probably mid-thirties. She looks frozen scared.

When I'm moved to an examining room and the nurse comes
through the open door, she seems hurried, all business. She's
probably in the middle of a treatment with another patient down
the hall. She has the single sheet of white paper from the printer.
She puts it inside the cover of my fat file. I can't read her face.

Droplets of sweat form on my scalp, in my armpits and on my back. The moment of truth. I want to snatch the paper from her. On her way out the door, she stops and looks at me. It hits her.

"You want to see it."

I can't speak.

"I guess it's all right. He'll be here soon to explain. You probably don't need much explanation."

She takes the paper from the folder, hands it to me, and then is gone. The critical count is at the top of the column. My eyes focus immediately on the little black number.

2.1.

It's up. Nowhere near normal, but *up* considerably from the last draw. The bottom end of normal is 3.8, but something positive is finally happening.

I get that rubbery feeling in my legs and am glad I'm not standing.

Twenty-two

In Chuck Palahniuk's Generation X novel, *Fight Club*, the protagonist, a young man bored with his unfulfilling but seemingly successful life, accompanies his risk-taking alter-ego, Tyler Durdan, to rob a convenience store. Tyler puts a gun to the clerk's head. Tyler seems psycho and likely to pull the trigger for the thrill of killing. The clerk is convinced he's living his last seconds. Tyler eventually lets him go and explains himself later by saying he gave the man a gift. The experience would cause him to appreciate his life more, cure him of his complacency.

Cancer cured me of depression.

Since I was a kid, black moods and thoughts of checking out had been an escape valve option that gave me a sense of control. When I found out I was sick, I felt as though I had a gun at my head. Now I was a walking dead man, bargaining for and trying to manage limited time, looking for the right balance between hope and acceptance. When the oncologist narrowed the diagnosis and we were reviewing my treatment options, I raised the question.

"What are my odds? I have two kids, eight and fourteen. Will I get to see them graduate from high school?"

"I don't know," he said. "Medical science is limited. We know some things and we're making progress, but there are no guarantees. I've been doing this a long time and have seen a lot of cases. This is your battle. We can help you fight it, but it's still your battle. My advice to you is to think positive. Plan to watch your children grow up; plan to survive. Make adjustments to your thinking when you must, and only then. Don't let yourself fall prey to what might be, until it actually is. We'll do our best to keep you alive and you must also do your part."

Then he gave me my treatment options. Interferon was the official silver bullet at the time. Interferon injections would likely give me flu-like symptoms, but could hold the cancer at bay and keep me alive. There was also this new treatment called cladribine (2-CDA) that was being tried at Scripps Institute in California. It was still considered experimental and hadn't been passed by the Food and Drug Administration. The results, so far, were very promising. Many of the test patients had achieved remission. Because I was reasonably young and otherwise healthy, I was a prime candidate to be part of the test group. He convinced me that it was my best choice by saying that if he was in my shoes, it was what he would do.

I had to sign a release, agreeing that neither I nor my family could hold the doctors, the drug company, the hospital, *anyone*, responsible if something went wrong. I was forced to acknowledge that I was desperate and this was a last-ditch effort.

I signed, and in the same moment decided that if I made it, I would go back to school. Before I found out I had cancer, I had started scheming, developing a plan to change jobs so I could be home with my family. When I was finishing college, the idea of being in charge of a classroom of high school kids was terrifying. To be an effective teacher, I would need to believe I had something worth passing on and I didn't have that belief then. Maybe I was ready now. My wife worked at our elementary school, so we knew how little beginning teachers made. We had been testing out living with the loss of pay, using the excess I made to pay down our mortgage. Without the cancer experience, I don't know if I would have had the courage to follow through. What we describe as courage is often desperation. The other options are even worse than being brave.

It took eight months, but by the following September, my health had improved. My blood counts had come up. The doctors felt that exposure to disease was less likely on the boat than in public places, and I started making tugboat trips.   When my immune system was at its weakest, my doctors had recommended against nursing home visits. In one of his war hallucinations, my father had injured himself and another patient. My sister, Lilly, had dealt with his hospital stay. He was now wheelchair bound and had been moved from the Alzheimer's ward to a less secure wing. The threat of him wandering off or getting in a fight had passed. My strength was returning and I was preparing to start school. I could visit him now.

As nursing homes go, Ascension has a good feel. There's tasteful artwork on the walls and built-in tanks with colorful tropical fish. It's clean and doesn't smell of urine or disinfectant. There's a sense of quiet, almost peace. My father's room was like a hospital room, minus the harsh lighting and plastic sterility, so it was also like a bedroom. When I arrived, an orderly was moving him from the bed to a wheelchair. It was his mealtime and he would be wheeled to the dining room. I was invited to go along.

He had lost weight, shrunk. It had been close to a year since I saw him last. When we admitted him, however crazy he was, he still had vitality and energy that made him a force to be reckoned with. Now he was withered and listless, a shell. He was mostly cooperative and when he spoke at all, it was only single words, nods or body stiffening to show disagreement, like a toddler who only knew a few words, but without toddler energy. He showed no sign of recognition, not even referring to me by his older brother's name. I had no sense that we were connecting.

The dining room was nearly empty, with only a few occupied tables, and we were given a private spot. The staff dealt with him daily and knew what to expect. They were being sensitive to my needs and whatever emotional adjustments I might be confronting, letting me discover his state for myself. On the way from his room I had been told that almost all of his food had to be puréed and he had to be fed. I was told which foods he would eat straight and how I'd have better luck with the vegetables if I added a touch of ice cream from the Dixie cup on the tray. To him, I was just today's feeder, today's orderly.

So I fed him and thought about how I'd rather the cancer got me than end up where he was. I thought about my mother, her cancer, and how she had warned me that when she could no longer go to the bathroom on her own, she was done, and how she had died before nightfall after the first day she needed help. I watched my father take in spoonfuls of different-colored mash with an exaggerated smacking sound similar to what I had heard at the dinner table when I was a kid.

His approval of my tugboat job had helped us connect. I doubt I would have gotten the same reaction to becoming a teacher. He believed colleges were infested with communists and homosexuals, and the rebellion inherent in my getting a degree went beyond just the student deferment. Now he was past the ability to comprehend and would likely be dead before I did my teaching internship. He would never know of this new phase in my life.

I thought about my sister, Kate, and her long-buried memories that had surfaced, and how she refused to be anywhere near him now.

Western Washington University had a graduate teacher certification program. I could commute to the campus from my home without moving my family. It took an effort, but I was able to meet the requirements, was accepted and could start school winter quarter. The tugboat company agreed to give me a leave to test the water. I worked on the boat from September until the end of December. I took out student loans. I refinanced my house. I was forty-three when first diagnosed, forty-four the winter I started school. My kids were now nine and fifteen. Instead of having to say goodbye, I was making a leap into unfamiliar space.

The campus at Western was populated with people who, with few exceptions, were much younger than me. I had been away longer than many of them had been alive. School was hard. It stretched me, made me grow, drained me. I made friends there, talked and listened. During the long walk alone from the commuter parking lot to Miller Hall, passing the rugby field and the new track where my daughter would later run, it would hit me, what I was doing, what I was living, and I would laugh out loud, amazed to be alive, starting over on a new adventure.

It took two years from start to finish, with summers back on the tugboats where they allowed me to continue working. My health seemed to be holding. The blood draws showed that my immune system was adequate and I was careful to get enough rest.

Student teaching was for me a total-immersion experience. The school where I did my internship was closer to home and a much easier commute than the university. The English department faculty there was wonderful. I felt accepted by them as a colleague and was fortunate to be assigned the perfect mentor who gave me both the freedom and support I required. I also had a good relationship with the supervisor from the college who had taught the most useful class I took there. I had great coaches, but it was still one of the hardest, most consuming things I've ever done.

Most of my own high school experience had happened during what I would have to describe as my nadir, the time when I was most disconnected, directionless and alone. It was not good. School is a structure where young people test themselves against a reflection of our society, with all its strengths and weaknesses, inconsistencies and faults. It's a good way to learn. By failing at high school, if you fail for the right reasons and learn from your failure, you can learn as much and become as successful later as you would by conforming and getting good grades. The doors just get harder to open.

I was older now and had built a life. I was a parent, had been married for more than twenty years, and knew how to get along with people who were very different from me. Tugboat life had built up my confidence and provided time to read and write. When I made the shift to mate, I experienced leading a crew of men. I now knew things that could be of value to young people finding their way into adulthood.

When I was called in for my routine intern interview with the vice-principal/dean of students, even though he was a nice man and easy to talk to, I had memories of other experiences in vice-principals' offices that hadn't gone so well. As a teacher-in-training, in high school once again, I feared I was an impostor. I trusted my ability to analyze and cut to the chase, to find the truth in the stories my classes would read, but I did not trust my filters or that I would know when to be tactful instead of blunt. This interview went fine, and I was learning that as I had changed, schools had grown too. I was finding that I could fit in.

I had to confront and get over my fear of speaking in public. I forced myself through it, and though I often sweated through my shirt while I was in front of the class, I tried to appear collected. I managed to perform. I like kids. They are looking for truth, for guidance. They are also looking for the easiest way and are good at finding the flaws and inconsistencies in people and institutions that have authority over them. I was good at rebelling against flawed authority too, and wanted to pass on what I had learned about how education and the skills you learn give you the power to say no to situations and organizations that want to control you.

The internship forced me through a transformation, a remodeling of me that the classes at Western had started but couldn't actually carry out. By engaging with a room full of kids, I became a teacher, something that I wasn't before, and all of it was good. It gave me hope.

Before the internship, during the time I was attending classes at Western, my blood counts had fluctuated, with key numbers usually hovering below the normal range but good enough for me to carry on with my life. Shortly after I began the internship, the counts started falling. The cancer was coming back. The blood counts got progressively worse. The "to be or not to be" debate in my body was heating up again.

The decline was slow, but steady. My doctor shortened the interval between exams, then shortened it again. I got my certificate in the mail, and went to work as a substitute in the school districts in my county. I stayed busy and was thankful for the challenge of confronting a room full of middle or high school kids whose names I hardly ever knew, trying to keep them focused on their work and my mind off of what was again happening in my body and where it might lead.

The doctor took another bone marrow sample. Not a dry tap this time, but not good news; half the blood cells were mutant. No big surprise. I was told that the disease would likely progress at a predictable pace and become critical the following winter. My options were the same as before, only now 2-CDA had been passed by the FDA and was the frontline drug for my brand of leukemia. I could take it again, and since I was in better health going in, this time it might work better. I decided that before going into the hospital for another round, I would continue substituting until June. In the coming fall the district where I was subbing the most would have a part-time opening for an English teacher. I applied for it, hoping I would be well enough when I needed to be.

Twenty-three

The first night in the hospital I shared a room with a man who I am certain was dying. He was there for a transfusion, new blood to buy him time. He was in pain. Pretreatment anxiety alone would have made for a restless night under the best of circumstances, but his groans and the frequent movement into and out of the room by the nurses kept me awake all night. His reality was likely my eventual future, and I vacillated between being afraid, feeling sorry for myself, and feeling fortunate that I still had hope. I suspect that my doctor assigned me to that room on purpose. I think he wanted me to spend the night reviewing my life and my reasons to fight for it.

I got a room to myself on the second day, when they started the chemo. The chemical is considered hazardous, and the nurses suit up in special gear to handle it. It would kill my blood, and I needed to be isolated because I would have no immune system. As part of the admitting process, they sent in a dietitian to find out if I had special food preferences or needs. I was honest, told them what I liked to eat. A big mistake. Between the chemo and the antibiotics, even with the anti-nausea drugs, all food became repulsive, and after the treatment was over, it took a while to get rid of the association between nausea and food I had previously liked.

The insertion of the PIC tube at the very beginning of the treatment forced me to accept that I was once again on the edge and leaping off into uncertainty, that I might die there in the hospital. The two women tasked with the job seemed nice, sympathetic, and they were asking me to trust them. It made me think of my horse and the look in his eyes when I helped the vet give him the lethal injection. I took some persuading before I let them push the tube into my arm, then through a vein over my shoulder and across my chest to one of the main veins that feeds my heart.

During the first few days of treatment, I still felt reasonably well. I had done it before. The 2-CDA was dripped in, around the clock. It would take seven days, then probably another week or so of hospital time. I could be upbeat when I talked to visitors, especially when they brought good news. The curriculum director and the superintendent from the district where I had applied stopped by to tell me I had the part-time job in the fall. The principal came in later to wish me well.

I read, watched TV, had visitors, dragged the IV units down the ward hall and back for exercise, showered with my arm wrapped in plastic to keep it dry, tubes running over the shower door to the wheeled stands. As my body grew weaker, I took advantage of my last chance to enjoy food before the plastic chemical taste and smell with its corresponding nausea made eating anything a challenge. I read a book about another calculated leap, Shackleton's voyage of exploration in the Antarctic. *Endurance* is an amazing story of survival and adventure in a place very different from the hospital setting of my current adventure. I read it nonstop until I was finished. It gave me hope.

After they had removed the last bag of 2-CDA, they gave me new blood. I thought I had made it through. Then the night nurse came in to take my temperature and blood pressure. I watched her face change as she read the thermometer. I asked her if it was serious.

She said, "It could be."

She left quickly and returned with some Ziploc bags full of ice. She told me to put them in my armpits and crotch. The bags were cold, damp, and unpleasant, but I didn't complain. I trusted her. She made me keep the thermometer in my mouth and she kept reading it. Then the ICU women came and put me on a gurney. I have fragmented memories of them taping a lot of wires to my arms, legs and chest, then hooking up the automatic blood pressure cuff and showing me how it worked so I wouldn't be startled, then I was gone.

The darkness is absolute. The room in ICU is framed through a rectangle, like a window. My body is on the bed below. The vantage points change from the ceiling above the bed to the wall near the ceiling, and I have no sense of time between changes. I feel no emotion as I watch myself in the bed below. I never focus on my face.

Now there are three doctors in green gowns standing in a huddle away from the bed. I hear no sound. They gesture, sometimes toward the monitor screens and then toward my body on the bed below me.

Snap! Something is messing with my arm. It's noisy. The automated blood pressure cuff on the left arm is pumping up to take its measurement. I'm freezing and I hurt all over. The doctors are looking at me as if I've come back from the dead. My oncologist breaks from the huddle and comes over.

"Am I glad to see you!" he says. The relief is genuine and emphatic.

It was the wee hours of the morning, an unusual time for a visit, but they told me that my wife was coming in. I caught on immediately. They brought a phone and I was able to dial our number. Allie's relief was clearly audible when she recognized my voice. I told her I was okay and she didn't need to come. She came anyway and sat with me while I wrote notes to the kids. When I was too weak to talk, she stayed, holding my hand.

It wasn't over. Though it got cold and shaky, I stayed in my body. Wires from probes regulated the temperature of water running through tubes between a machine and the plastic blanket I was wrapped in, keeping my body from overheating. My heart-

beat became irregular, randomly racing at times. They ran an
EKG and gave me some pills that eventually worked. I tried to
meditate, but couldn't focus. When I was conscious, I was cold—
teeth-chattering, bone-shaking cold.

On the old tugboat where I was chief engineer for thirteen
years, I had a survival suit lashed above my bunk in such a way
that I could pull a string and it would fall on my chest. The steel
hull was getting punky, and there were places below the waterline that were pretty thin. If there was trouble, I thought I could
get out through a porthole or one of the steel doors at either end
of the passageway outside my stateroom. I planned to get the
survival suit on quickly, but I sometimes imagined what it would
be like to float in that cold Pacific water for days until someone
came or you died. I don't wonder anymore.

"Are you sure you'll be all right?" she asks.

"I can do this," I say. "I'm okay."

*This part of the hospital seems empty, out of service. In the dark-
ness, the shower is a bright enclave that includes a place to dress. I feel
fragile and am glad I don't have to interact with anyone but the nurse.
There are beds in the shadows, and the lighting in the ward feels soft,
amber, unusual for the hospital where everything is always so well-lit
and florescent sterile. The stall tiles are that yellow-orange and there's a
built-in ledge if I need to sit. The nurse runs the water until it's warm,
then shuts it off.*

"I'll stay where I can hear. If you're having trouble, let me know."

*I pull the opaque glass door closed. If she's watching, she can see my
head above it. I don't mind. She seems to understand, and after being
helpless, depending on oncology nurses, I've let go of modesty about my
body and its functions. She left fresh pajamas and two towels. As I slide
the neatly folded stack to where I think it will stay dry, I can feel that
it has been warmed. I grasp the chrome handle, cool and smooth, adjust
the water temperature, get out of the backless hospital gown and step*

under the stream.

The water hits my head and face. The flow of warmth startles me as it runs down my body, defining the shape of my torso and legs. I'm struck by how foreign is this shape I seem to have re-inhabited. It's definitely the same body I left. The scars on my arm, knees and right leg are all in the right places. The lower back stiffness didn't disappear, but the disconnect is profound. I shampoo my hair and feel the waxy crust that has formed in the crease behind my ears.

I'm still wobbly. I steady myself against a shower wall.

I got stronger. When the fever left, they moved me back to a regular hospital room. Then I bounced back. It wasn't much more than a week after leaving the ICU that they let Allie bring me down the stairs from my room to sit with her outdoors. A remodeling project had started and the courtyard was being dug up, but the machinery was gone that afternoon and we were alone in the relative quiet. The trip down the stairs was a huge effort. As I rested on the bench, feeling the simple sensations of sun on my face, the moving air and the absence of hospital smell, I had another one of those involuntary experiences that print indelibly in memory. Quietly, holding Allie's hand, I let hope back in. I let myself realize I was alive and a future might be possible.

It was as if I had been purged, as if the debate in my body had gotten violent, then decisive. With the help of new drugs, my blood counts improved. They let me out for a few hours one day, and Allie drove me home. I ate a bowl of plain white rice at our dining room table because it was the only food that I could face without wanting to vomit. I sat under the poplars on the deck in our backyard and believed again in the reality of home and tomorrow.

I went back to the hospital, but was released a few days later. They left the PIC tube in my arm, just in case. When, after a few more weeks, they took it out, my confidence got another boost. Recovery from the first treatment had taken months. I had spent weeks on the couch, staring through a double-hung window casement at the backside of a shrub. I had no energy. Loading the washing machine required an hour's nap for recovery. A walk around the block was a major milestone, and it was several months before I could ride my bicycle any significant distance.

This time it was different.

The first walk around the block was shaky, but within a few days I was walking several blocks. The first bicycle ride was wobbly and dangerous because I was dizzy. I got over it and pushed the distances farther and farther. Within a month I had ridden to the river and back. When school started, I was ready. As I regained my strength, I started adding to my part-time assignment by using free hours to fill in for teachers who needed coverage.

I liked getting up in the morning, and though they were often exhausting, I liked most of my days. By my second year, I was given a full schedule of classes. The job suited me well. The first few years were almost as hard as the internship. My health fluctuated, set off alarms. The doctor shortened times between check-ups, then lengthened them again. But I also had a few blood counts that were normal across the board. Important as anything else that was happening to me, the bouts of depression I'd experienced since childhood were gone. The anti-suicide team inside me debated well, and its regime is in power, for now.

Twenty-four

As the peroxide foams on the angry pulp of the gravel scrape on his knee, my son lets out a wail that could be heard by someone passing in the street. I squeeze the cotton ball dry and tilt the bottle to saturate a new one. It's a bad scrape, embedded with dirt, and he's letting me know how much it stings. He fell, riding his bicycle at a friend's house, when another kid stopped too fast in front of him. He says he didn't cry then because he didn't want to be a baby in front of his friends. He's making up for it now. He's learning that treating the wound can be more painful than the original wounding, and he's having to accept my word that enduring some pain now will save him from more later.

The rest of his body is writhing in full complement to the noise he's making, but the knee stays still and I finish applying the peroxide. The knee and his elbow will need to be soaked in the tub with Epsom salts and I know it won't happen without a battle.

"I'm not taking a bath!"

I've just told him that he'll need to get in the tub and his response pretty much guaranties that today is the day we deal with both his fear of pain, and his fear of the tub falling down with him in it.

"Why not?" I say.

When he was small he wouldn't take showers because he didn't like the sting of being pelted with water. He changed his mind when one of the clawed feet of the old bathtub came loose and the tub tipped with him in it. It didn't tip over or even tilt to where the unsupported corner touched the floor. It just got tippy and no longer felt solidly anchored. He has an active imagination and hasn't had a bath since. We haven't pushed it because learning to take showers was a positive step.

"I'm not taking a bath. I hate baths. I'll take a shower."

I can see from his eyes that he knows his logic is shaky, and that being afraid won't be good enough, but I also know he has a stubborn streak that rivals my own, and I'd better be careful. I resort to scare tactics. "You need to soak," I say. "If you don't soak it, it will get infected. Then it will get worse and you'll have to soak it three times a day and put even more peroxide on it. If you do it now, it will probably heal and you won't have to do it any more." I'm loosing patience. My wife helps out by saying,

"You can't still be afraid that the tub will fall down. Daddy fixed that when it happened and it's fine now."

"No way. I'm not doing it."

We're tapping into his stubborn streak and I'm getting enough of it. The tub legs aren't bolted on and can be knocked loose if they're bumped hard enough or often enough, but it's only happened once in twenty years. But it happened when he was in the tub, so I go to the bathroom and check them.

"The legs are fine," I say when I return.

"Oh sure. Did you weld them on or just put them back so they can fall down again."

"Are you calling me a liar?" It's the wrong thing to say and I know it, but I'm exasperated and it just came out.

"Sort of," he says with a hint of a smirk that lets me know that the situation isn't quite out of control yet.

"Go soak your wounds," I say.

"I'm not doing it!" he says and storms out of the room, slamming the door behind him. I start to follow and my wife lets me know with a look that maybe I haven't screwed it up yet but if I go through that door I probably will, and it's her turn now. So I get out of the way and she follows him up the stairs to his room where they will negotiate a settlement and eventually he will end up in the tub. She'll take the time to talk him through his fear. He knows that if he doesn't work it out with her, he will have to face me and it will go all wrong. I'm hoping that the threat will help rather than hinder.

My son will be running in a race today. I'm sitting in Fairchild Stadium, a high school sports stadium, named for Colin Fairchild, who is now dead. When I was a child, he was the groundskeeper here at Gethsemane. My sister, Lilly, is sitting next to me. Decades ago, she graduated from this school. A few weeks ago, she went to Mrs. Fairchild's funeral. I was also invited to the funeral, but I didn't go. This morning, when a wreck on I-5 near Everett threatened to make me late to the track meet, I realized that I had delayed leaving home because I dreaded being in this place again.

It's a nice stadium for a small school, a definite improvement over the field that was outside my father's print shop on the flat ground above the hill behind me. As a small boy, I watched uniformed big boys practice football in the same purple and gold colors the Ascension track athletes are wearing today. The old field now lies underneath the nursing home where my father died after sharing residence in D-Wing with Mrs. Fairchild, who outlasted him by several years and also had Alzheimer's disease. There is a radio transmission tower next to the nursing home. I remember when its predecessor was being built and the athletic field was moved down here, replacing the old pig and chicken sheds, the slaughterhouse and the mechanic's shop.

The white, open-sided tent for the timers and spotters on the infield near the track finish line is at about the same spot where farm sheds were once clustered. Old pictures interfere, and the intrusions impose an unreal quality on the track meet I've come to watch.

My father moves the little ones in the pen so that the mother won't roll

*over and crush them. The sow, massive quivering fat, pink and black, lies
on a bed of straw. The tiny piglets squirm around the swollen teats on
her sagging belly. The bloody puddle of afterbirth is still on the ground
near the sow's tail and my father picks it up with a shovel and carries
it out of the shed. The sow makes low, grunting noises and her breath
comes hard. I want to touch her and to touch the piglets, but my father
won't let me in the pen with them.*

*I squat silently behind a bush in the tall grass along the lane that leads
up to the dirty, whitewashed building. I hear gunshots and pig squeals
from inside. I move to where I can see the men bind each pig's hind feet
together and raise the carcass with a block and tackle so that it hangs
from a hook on a rail that runs across the slaughterhouse ceiling. The
dead pigs are lined up in a row, upside down. I watch the blood run out
over my father's hands as he cuts the pigs' throats with a knife.   The
blood drains into a trough built into the slaughterhouse floor. The three
pigs look asleep as my father and the other man slit their bellies and
remove their guts.*

*When their work with the pigs is finished, they hose the blood and
slime off the concrete floor. I wait until they're gone and when I'm sure
no one is watching, I go through the open door and squat by the head
of the first pig. Its open eyes are blank and empty. Blood oozes from the
mouth and nostrils. Buzzing flies hover and land, darting around the
eyes and mouth.*

*I touch its nose. It feels rubbery and strange. Panic strikes. I run
from the building into the sunlight and the tall grass where a cool breeze
is blowing. I push my way through the grass, which is nearly as tall as
I am, until I'm away from the slaughterhouse. I trample the stalks in a
small area, making a place like a room with no roof, and lie down. I pull
a stalk of grass and chew the end, watching the blotchy clouds move
across the sky.*

On the hill above that end of the field is the remodeled version of what was once the boys' dorm. The old gym was inside. To the right of the boys dorm, looming above the crest of the steep bank that surrounds the field on three sides, is the concrete-and-brick, fortress-like structure of the powerhouse. It is imposing, neo-gothic, and several stories tall. It housed the big furnaces that heated the water that produced the steam that warmed all the buildings. The furnaces burned continually in cold weather, and what I saw through the vents in the large cast-iron furnace doors inspired a vision in my imagination of the lake of fire where I might spend eternity.

I would go there through the tunnels from the Monarch Building, which is still behind me, beyond the trees, near the new nursing home. Before the rolling lawns were covered with new buildings, the long boxy fortress of the Monarch stood out for its plainness among the formal gardens, fishponds, and stately Tudor architecture. I would push a hand truck through the tunnels that had the dual uses of piping the steam heat and providing sheltered passage for the dying. I exchanged used lead type for the lead ingots that were raw material for the old Linotype in my father's print shop.

The broad avenue leading to the Administration Building hasn't changed much. It looks exclusive. It's still as imposing to the uninvited, the outsider, as it probably once was to the patient. Today, even though the outside streets were lined with cars, there were many open spaces on the Av. I knew from when my father was in the nursing home that I could have parked there without being towed, yet, unwilling to face nursing home memories, I drove past, found parking on a side street and walked a little farther to get to the stadium.

My son is sitting next to me, wearing the green uniform of his team, our team. I teach at his school. We find his race in the program and check his record time against the times of his competitors. This is an important track meet, tri-district. The top three in each event go on to the state championships in Cheney next weekend. Based on the times, he decides that he will probably be running for sixth place, which will still earn a medal.

I'm proud of him for getting this far in his first year. He's a junior, but chose drama rehearsals over track and had a role in the spring play each of the past two years. It took him a while at the beginning of the season to find his event, the 400, but he's worked hard at it, and his times have improved enough to get him here and give me this day in this place. The neighbor girl, who runs in the women's 400, draws him away to warm up. I watch them stretching on the grass infield not far from the site of the old slaughterhouse.

Among the advertisements for local businesses on the chain-link fence around the stadium, I see the slogan, "Go Crusaders," and remember back when a lighted field for home games at night had to be rented. There were no covered stands with aluminum bleachers as I rode my horse ahead of the team onto the field at Henderson Park. I was in fifth or sixth grade, hadn't gone completely bitter yet, and allowed my sister who was on some high school committee to talk me into it. They dressed me as a page and dressed the horse up in purple and gold too, like a crusader's horse. We flew a big flag, probably made in home-ec class, with a C on it. The flag, on a staff supported in a boot I made for it and attached to the stirrup, fluttered and whipped above my head. It had scared the horse at first and he took some soothing and practice before he accepted it. The crowd, too, made him jumpy, but he got used to that also.

Between the dorm and the powerhouse, I can see the top of a yellow school bus parked back from the edge of the bank. When my father was dying here, I took my family to show them the tiny apartment that, in the TB days, had been nurses' quarters. It was up beyond the boys' dorm, across the street from the powerhouse. The building is gone now. Our communal front yard, where the old playhouse once was, is the bus parking lot, but the concrete slab that was under the row of narrow one-story units remains, and I was able to show them the outline of the few tiny rooms where the six of us had lived.

The apartments were between the boys' and girls' dorms. A covered wooden ramp met our building a few feet to the right of our front door and, after passing the entrance to the girls' dorm, it rose over the street to connect with the basement of the stately building that housed the high school and chapel on the hill above. The ramp allowed us access to the tunnels, and when it rained we could walk to most of the other buildings on the compound without getting wet. The ramp, too, is gone now. Beyond the low wooden structure of the girls' dorm, there were trees, lawn, and a cement wading pool.

The wading pool is covered over by Thurmond Auditorium. Mrs. Thurmond was my third grade teacher. I don't remember any warmth. My father's memorial service was held in the auditorium and I am invited there to an old-boy reunion each summer, but never go. At the memorial service, I found satisfaction in watching my sister, Lilly, her husband and her two grown kids confidently sit in the row next to the church deacon who had sent her the letter that had forced her to choose between church membership and the path that led to the existence of that family.

During the reception after the service, at the refreshment table, my daughter was asked whom she was related to. When she identified me, the person said that her mother must be pretty amazing, implying that taming me was quite an accomplishment. It's true, her mother is pretty amazing, but probably not in the way implied.

Beyond the auditorium, on the side of the hill above what was the playfield, lies the building where I went to grade school. It's made of concrete and brick and looks a little like the powerhouse.

The road came around the Ad Building from the big, landscaped circle at the main entrance and past the rear service access for the kitchen where I had gone in to get the ice cream. I was returning from the main kitchen in the Ad Building with Sunday dinner dessert for my family, and it surprised me that I was alone.

There were six scoops in the tray, one for each of us. They were vanilla, peppermint candy and chocolate, and I had to hurry so they wouldn't melt. The metal ice cube tray was cold in my hands. The grade school building where I went to Sunday school was on the downhill side of the road, on my right. I was where the buses lined up before and after school, which I was still too young to go to, but it was Sunday and there was no one around.

The sunlight was bright and golden on everything and the grass seemed too green. There was a cement retaining wall on the high side of the road and above it a lawn, then, like a structure from a fairy tale, the high school building with the chapel inside. The cement of the roadway was seamed and cracked. I felt something that made me look away from the ice cream and up toward the high school building. The white bear was standing on the grass, stone still and magnificent. I froze as still as it stood, and stared. The claws were ivory, stained with brown, and I could see them as though they were as close as the ice cream. The white fur was golden in the sunlight and moved lightly in the breeze. The teeth were smooth and white and the bear had brown eyes that were fixed on me. The eyes were looking through me and I knew they could see into my soul. They weren't angry. They were big and clear and piercing and seemed close, and the white bear stood motionless, looking through me, and I couldn't stand it.

I ran.

On the sidewalk in the shadows under the ramp there was a man with a girl standing beside him. The girl was older than me and I had never talked to her. The man was her father and they lived in the Ad Building in an apartment upstairs. I would have run by, but they called to me. I stopped.

"What's the hurry?" the father said. "You've spilled your ice cream."
"Bear," was all I could say.
"Where?" the father said. "There are no bears around here."
"Back there. By the high school," I said.
"Show me," the father said, not believing.

I was afraid, but I led them back. The bear was nowhere in sight. I expected it to surprise us from a different direction. Another man was coming down the sidewalk from the wood shop, and we met him where the sidewalk met the road. There was a pile of rubble on the ground that hadn't been there before.

While the girl's father was asking the man if he had seen the bear, I looked at the pile on the sidewalk. It was the bear. The magnificent, terrible eyes were gone. The head was completely gone and the body was mutilated, like the body of a dog that has been repeatedly run over on a busy highway. There was fur in the pile, dirty and matted, and something that looked like canned salmon. It stank. It was the bear; I was certain of it. The men were talking and paying no attention to me or to the pile on the ground.

"It's the bear," I said, pointing at the pile.

The men ignored me and kept talking. I waited and watched the flies landing on the pile. Finally, the father turned to me and said, "Shouldn't you go home and explain about the ice cream? There are no bears around here." Then he turned back to the other man and resumed talking.

I rarely remember dreams, but this one has never left me.

My son and his friend are still warming up. His teammates in their green and white Eagles uniforms come and go around me in the stands. They all are, or have been, my students, so I'm not here just for my son's race. Their parents encourage them, share their pre-race anxiety, praise the winners and console those who miss out on the glory. I watch their races and encourage and console too. I look beyond where my son jogs around the infield, past the fenced edge of the stadium into what was once a densely wooded valley. I drove down there after a visit to my father; it has also changed. The rustic cabin and picnic area have been replaced by new school buildings. The trails where I rode Scout after we moved off grounds are gone.

On a stand in the infield directly in front of where we are sitting, the medals are awarded as the track events are completed. There are many purple and gold Ascension uniforms on the risers, often in the top three. It is becoming clear that the Ascension Crusaders are doing quite well and will probably win the meet and send a large group to state. The school has a reputation for high academic standards and their sports teams often do well. The kids seem to have the confidence of preppie privilege, and the parents look as successful as their kids. A few standouts from our school will win state berths, but most of our kids will have to be satisfied with beating their own best performance so far.

Earlier my sister identified the Crusaders' rooting section to see if there was anyone she recognized. As winners are announced, we listen for familiar names, and she comments that many of the kids would have different last names from the adults we're trying to connect them with. I wondered aloud how many of the adults who grew up here with us could afford the tuition. It has become the kind of place that well-off parents send their kids to keep them safe from the dangers of public schools.

My parents had high ideals and gave up material possessions to come here. We who lived here shared what we had with each other and with other people in need. The place was run like a commune. Each family got a certain amount of grocery credit to use at a commissary where the food had been donated, obtained as government surplus, or bought cooperatively in bulk. We got our clothing from a big room in the basement of one of the main buildings that had charity clothes on shelves and racks, like a thrift store. Our family got $50 in actual cash each month as an allowance for things that required money. The adults used the skills they brought to advance the cause, and developed new skills as the cause required. There was daycare and supervised play for us kids. *Perfect communism in the garden of the Lord from a group of people who equated communism with devil worship.*

When I was thirteen, my father quit working at Gethsemane in a dispute over money. His low wages didn't trouble him. The administrators wanted him to use the print shop as a business and make money to help finance the rest of the operation. He thought the shop should focus on low-cost service to missionaries. The differences were eventually patched, and he returned several years later to work here at a competitive wage with a medical plan until he retired. When we admitted him to the nursing home, it was the first time I had been back since they kicked me out at the end of sixth grade. Even back then, they had a waiting list of kids whose parents could pay. I didn't bring in tuition and caused enough trouble to override the embarrassment of giving up on one of their own.

Back at the track meet, our star girl has won both the high jump and the 100-meter hurdles. A girl from my first period class, one of my son's classmates, is running the mile. Like my son, she's going for a personal record rather than a trip to state. My son is next to me in the stands, getting his spikes. He looks worried. I catch his eye.

"I've got a side ache," he says. "This is something new."

"Go stretch some more," I say. "See if you can work it out."

I can see that I'm not much help. He grabs the running shoes and goes. I hope it's just nerves and feel a sympathetic knot forming in my gut. I want him to be successful. I would love to see him win, go to state, be a star, but what I really want is for him to know that he's run his best race and to learn that it's worthwhile to do that, even though someone will always come along who is faster or stronger.

There's a runner from Ascension in his race and I wonder if the boy's parents are praying for him to win, like the group of Ascension parents we sat near at a state meet several years ago where we had gone to watch our daughter run and jump. At first I resented their arrogance. How dare they assume favor from God for their children over other children. What kind of a god would do that anyway? Success and safety from failure in the garden of the Lord. *Father, forgive them, for they know not what they do.*

My father claimed to be forgiven. He clung to life that last year when he couldn't even chew his own food. Was it the biology and chemistry of the disease winning out over spirit? He was stuck in the perfect living hell, helpless, without a shred of dignity. Bliss through perfect ignorance? Or, was his hanging on an expression of an internal struggle? Maybe he didn't trust his reservation in heaven.

While he was in E-Wing, I was fighting leukemia, changing careers. It was my big test, my chance to do my personal best. He died while I was studying Greek mythology, learning about Priam and Achilles, each grieving personal loss in the midst of a war over the ownership of beauty. And now, I'm down here in the stands at Fairchild Stadium, an arena named after one of my father's friends, and I'm watching my son set up his starting blocks, remove his warm-ups and take his mark.

The starter raises his pistol, fires, and they're off running. My son is tall, thin and muscular. He runs gracefully, but so do the others. The pack spreads a little, but it remains a close race around the final bend and into the home stretch. He's found sixth and is holding his place as he passes in front of me. I watch as, in the final 50 yards his legs turn to lead, he loses his grace, and must force his body on. The runner behind him has just enough left to squeak by and take the bottom medal from him as they finish.

I can see his disappointment from here. It was a tight race all the way, and at the finish line there was still only a short span between the first- and last-place runners. At least he didn't get blown away. I know that the exertion has made him feel like throwing up. The neighbor girl is there with him, and they walk past the tent where the slaughterhouse was. They cross the infield toward the fence that separates the stadium from the wooded ravine below it. They pass over the place where nearly half a century ago, I had my first memorable experiences with birth and death. They'll walk and jog, powering down, until he is called to the risers to have his place announced, and to feel the humiliation of not receiving a medal. I feel bad for him, but know there is nothing I can do.

When his place is called, he walks to the riser. He seems to have recovered his poise and stands with dignity, which makes me proud. It's not long before he's in the stands. He silently threads his way up the bleachers between spectators and sits next to me. I hesitate, then look at him and ask,

"How was the side ache?"

"I stretched some more and it went away before the race."

"So, how do you feel now?"

"I ran out of gas at the end and he passed me, but I beat my best time by a full second."

The improvement allows him to accept the defeat. I'm thankful and proud too that I get to be his father.

It's been a tough year for all of us. Now it's graduation night, and you can feel it in the air. One of our students disappeared. Hundreds of green and white helium filled balloons form an arch above the graduates and a huge banner tells the year. Their families sit in the rows of folding chairs set up on either side of the arches made from cedar boughs woven into wire frames that decorate the center aisle. Potted plants and bouquets of irises beautify the raised, portable stage.

Teachers sit on the opposite side of the stage from the graduates. We look across the open space in front of the podium at them and at the bleachers on that side. Those are the closest seats not reserved for family. Usually, they are occupied by kids with strong connections to the graduates, and who want a good view. I'm surprised to see a girl from one of my classes, Natalie, sitting alone in the top row. She's already had to say a hard good-bye. The girl who disappeared was her best friend, Kristen.

Kristen's car was found abandoned in the mall parking lot, but what happened remains a mystery. They arrested a boy named Corey on evidence she had been with him at a campsite out by the river. He admits she was there, but it was a week before, and he denies knowing anything about her disappearance. His account hasn't wavered, and they finally had to release him, but everyone thinks he killed her. He was probably safer locked up.

I've read both his and Kristen's journals and don't believe he could have hurt her. I thought I saw an unlikely friendship developing between them. He's been in trouble and done some stupid things, but I believe if he knows anything about what happened to Kristen, he would have told the police right away. The town, the school, everyone wants an answer, and pinning it on Corey would make people feel safer, but it feels wrong to me.

I believe Corey is innocent and I can relate to the danger of the dark place he's in. When my professor friend believed in me, it changed my life. It may have been a stupid move, and I haven't told anyone except Allie, but I offered Corey the money I got from selling a boat. It isn't much, but it might be a way for him to get away from here and start fresh. Corey hasn't asked for it yet, but maybe knowing I believe him is a help to him.

My bond with Allie and our kids keeps me fighting. I think the connection I get from teaching, the involvement in my students' lives, is also a big part of what keeps the cancer at bay.

Twenty-five

When I was in junior high, at my most troubled, I had friends whose parents were drunks, and I wasn't sure whether alcoholism was worse than my father's way. More than the occasional backhand across my face, it was the sense of rejection, the loss of his love that I ended up hating him for. I needed his help, trying to solve the problems of growing up, trying to find my moral compass, and he made it worse. His answer was always to ask the Lord. No matter how hard I tried, and I did try, I could never feel the connection to whatever it was he was praying to.

But he kept the horse.

Scout was our link, our common ground, the connection that neither of us could break. At my father's house, Scout earned his keep. He was ridden and loved by neighbor kids and grandkids and was still there when I finally had my own kids. Scout grew old, and a lump developed on his lower jaw at the back near where it hinged. The lump was small at first and didn't appear to hurt him. He just looked funny, like a lopsided chipmunk, or like he had the mumps. The lump grew. The vet diagnosed bone cancer. There was no cure.

The call came and before he actually said it, I knew from my father's voice. Scout was starving to death. They had been feeding him painkillers to enable him to chew, but the lump had now grown big enough to prevent him from opening his mouth. I called the vet who agreed to meet me there later that day.

When I joined my brother and the horse in the field, Scout recognized me. He looked sad and wise. I bawled like a baby, like I

did when my mother died. It surprised me; I couldn't stop it. My
father found me that way, hugging the horse's neck, blubbering.
Through all the grief of the last twenty-six years, the horse had
been a fixture in my life, and now it came rushing out from wher-
ever I had been storing it. When my father's eyes met mine, the
same thing happened to him.

I tied Scout to a tree near the spot where we had decided to
dig the grave. We dug through the roots and rocks in the red dirt
with a pick and shovels. The work helped, but when one of us
looked up at the horse or just thought about what we were doing,
it would hit again, and the other one would catch it. My brother,
David, who was helping and understood enough of it, caught it
too.

For a birthday gift when I was a boy, my parents gave me an
expensive, leather-covered bible with pictures. The picture at the
beginning of the book was of Isaac bound hand and foot, clearly terrified, lying over some sticks of wood on a rock altar. His
anguished father, Abraham, was standing over him, clasping a
raised dagger, ready to pierce Isaac's heart. In the background
there was an angel, and tangled in a leafless bramble bush, a lamb
was waiting to be discovered. I knew the story well and had no
doubts that my father, like Abraham, would kill me for his God,
and to his God, I believed I was just a means for testing my father's commitment. I wasn't aware of any lamb in the bushes
waiting to come to my rescue.

Maybe the horse was the angel and the lamb rolled together.
Without this horse, I couldn't have ridden his horse after it threw
him. Without the horses, the barrier that had emerged between us
would have become an impenetrable wall.

We blubbered and dug, and by the time we heard the vet's
van pull up to the house, we had gone deep enough. I could just
see over the edge of the hole. My father and brother went to the
house and waited, leaving me alone with the horse and the vet.

I held Scout while the vet found the vein. Scout knew something was up and struggled, making it hard to give the shot. The drug worked quickly. His legs gave out and he went down. I sat on the ground holding his head. I could feel his breathing slow as the barbiturate did its job. The vet waited long enough to be sure he had injected enough. Then he left us alone.

I felt Scout die. His body stayed warm after his breathing stopped. I couldn't help thinking that if he had a spirit or soul, it was leaving then, and I hoped it understood why we had given him the shot. Then I started thinking about a movie I had seen. Some Bushmen in the Kalahari Desert in Africa had hunted and killed a giraffe. They had used a dart with a slow-acting poison, and they had to track the wounded giraffe for days.

Too sick to go farther, the giraffe finally took a stand. The little men had to dash in close, under the giraffe's legs, and it tried to kick them as they killed it with crude spears. It was a life-or-death struggle for both the men and the giraffe, and the men won. When the giraffe was dead, they had a ceremony before the butchering, thanking its spirit for the life it had given them by dying. As I knelt beside Scout's body, I thanked his spirit for the part he had played in my life.

When my father and brother returned we tried to drag the body to the grave and couldn't. It was too heavy. My father got the tractor and some rope. I put my jacket over Scout's head to cover his eyes. The body didn't land right in the hole. I went in to straighten it and make it look at rest. Again, it was too heavy. I retrieved my jacket and covered his head with a worn saddle blanket that a friend of my parents had sent as a gift when I was a boy.

When I climbed out of the grave, my father and brother stood waiting, and I realized that this was the moment when, at a funeral, the minister or priest would pray, so – and this was a huge step for me – I asked my father to pray.

I don't know how he interpreted it. I don't know if he thought that I was finally breaking down, seeing the light and on the road to salvation, and I don't care. He had a name and words he could use that felt true to him. The best I could do was a mental image of some Bushmen and a giraffe, and though that was almost good enough, there was a need for something to be said, a ritual, a formality, an official farewell to a noble spirit that we had both loved and respected.

My father stood in the woods next to the hole we had dug together and spoke to his god about Scout as though the horse were a venerable man. For that day, or that moment at least, we were not fighting over who owned the truth, and in spite of our very real and deep sorrow for each other, we were equal in our deliverance. Our gratitude and grief were shared honestly and truly, and the world was a more hopeful place.

And then we buried the horse. My brother's wife planted ferns and trilliums on the grave and later I made a marker out of oak.

Twenty-six

Fifteen years before Kate's recovered memory, her husband committed suicide. He left her emotionally stretched with two small children, the youngest an infant. Her decisions often seemed frantic, impulsive. Her money disappeared. Life had dealt her a bad hand and she rewarded herself in ways I thought imprudent. We had all tried to help, but my father, being retired, had come through most often, taking the kids sometimes for days, covering for her when she was overwhelmed. Her account of a recovered memory came out in installments, eventually revealing her new conviction that our father was evil. To us, her new belief was surprising.

While Kate needed to publicly assassinate our father's character, the rest of us tried to take it in. We each had experienced our father in our own way, and we clung to and protected our personal stories, our separate experiences of him. We were focused on taking care of an old man with Alzheimer's. Her outrage at our father seemed to reassign the blame she had directed at the doctors and psychiatrists who had failed her husband. Life had wronged her and it was someone's fault. No one tried to shut her down or challenge or ostracize her. We just didn't respond much at all.

The idea of repressed memory has been around since Sigmund Freud. Both its existence and accuracy are controversial even today, and at the time Kate's memory was returning, the controversy was building to a peak. Proponents believe that repressed memories can be recovered, usually spontaneously, years or decades after the event.

Most psychologists maintain it's also possible to construct convincing pseudo-memories for events that never occurred, that, through suggestion, therapy can create false memories that may be a blend of actual memories and outside influences. Courts are still reluctant to admit recovered memory without other corroborating evidence.

We were back home after an excursion to the post office, a walk over the hill and back. Besides getting something necessary done, it was a way to get out of the house.

He had been agitated the whole time, which stressed me out. He said that we were going the wrong way, that Aunt Sara was having trouble with her well and we needed to go there to fix it. I started out arguing that Aunt Sara didn't live around here and we were just going to the post office. That made him angry and he tried to leave. Eventually it occurred to me that this was a moment when I could try following my brother's advice. Maybe by listening to him and by using the story he was living, I could get his cooperation. I told him we would go to Aunt Sara's after we got the mail, that she was waiting for a package and we needed to see if it had arrived.

He was suspicious but we got the mail (no package for Sara, maybe tomorrow) and made it back to the house. Then I told him Sara had sent a message. Someone else had stopped by and got the well problem fixed. He wanted to know who it was. I didn't even know who Aunt Sara was, so I said Allie hadn't told me, and then asked who he thought it might have been. I didn't know that person either.

We were sitting on the couch. Allie came in and said something about Kate. Dad recognized the name and said,

"I haven't seen Kate for a long time. Is she still around?"

"Yeah, but she has to take a ferry to visit, so we don't see as much of her as we'd like. She's mad at you."

"Oh?"

"She says you hurt her when she was little."
"Oh?"
"She says you molested her."
There was a pause.
"We played around a little, but there was never any penetration."
Two short phrases presented like an aside in a play, another message from behind the wall. By the time I took it in, he was on an agitated mission to find his glasses, which he was wearing. That same day he reported seeing cars on the neighbors' roof and giant geese attacking a calf in a field.

When the nursing home called to say his body was finally shutting down, it wasn't a surprise. He wouldn't last more than a few days without intrusive life support. He had been stubbornly hanging on. I had signed the document rejecting life support. He had been clear about that. They were verifying, giving me the chance to change my mind. It was a strange moment, like signing the waiver to let them test the leukemia drug on me. On the one hand it was a weighty decision; on the other, it was no decision at all.

I confirmed that nature should be allowed to take its course, and they told me they would keep him as comfortable as possible with morphine. The frail shell that was my father would soon stop breathing. Not yet dead, he was lying in state. We had a few days to view him, to say goodbye, to attempt to make peace before the last trace of life left the body and it was interred.

Only the bed was illuminated. The rest of the room seemed dark. My father was lying on his back, drugged, unresponsive, asleep, a dark blue blanket with a neatly folded sheet covering all but his head and shoulders. His eyes were closed. He looked small and absent, the way bodies appear in caskets.

When my horse, Scout, died, I was holding his head, and the moment remains clear. I felt something powerful depart and my sense of loss at its absence was intense and profound. My father cried with me that day. His grief came from a true place within him, and our sharing it clarified for us the complexity of our love for each other and its accompanying anguish. In the hospital now, I studied his face. Instead of grief, I felt disorientation.

He had told me he'd seen demons and he was certain that the devil existed. If the judgment he believed in was real, the big moment was at hand. He was done stalling and would soon be facing his Lord.

Images of our past together flashed through my mind. I pictured him praying by the bed after he let me hit him. I saw him thanking me for riding the horse that threw him, and after I flunked the draft physical, stopping me from leaving his house. I saw him crying while we buried Scout. I wondered if he was now looking down on this scene.

Images of him with my sister when she was a child tried and failed to form. I couldn't visualize or couldn't allow myself to visualize what, "we played around a little, but there was no penetration" meant.

I made a loud sound that I can only describe as visceral, animal, beyond words.

To carry on with life, people who have been wronged somehow have to make peace. Kate wanted more than validation. She wanted revenge. The ancient Greeks embraced retribution as a way to find justice, to even the scales. It was part of their ethos. If you didn't meet your obligation to avenge a wrong, you were haunted by the Furies. In the Old Testament, the Israelites refer to it as "an eye for an eye." Fear of retribution was a deterrent.

Kate would have publicly crucified our father if she had had the chance. When we didn't embrace her view, she felt betrayed. I remembered what it felt like to look in the mirror the night I loaded the gun. I remembered his eyes when I hit him the second time. To be free, she needed him to apologize. She needed to see him cry. He eventually read a novel manuscript I wrote, recognized it as the thinly disguised account of real events that it was and cried as he handed it back to me, saying he was sorry. I didn't share Kate's need for revenge.

Our father was now as broken as a person can get. Any dignity was gone. What could you take away from him but the image of him other people remembered? Who would that help and who would it damage? It could backfire and hurt Kate more than anyone else. I had found a doorway, a path through my hate and disappointment toward him. She needed validation. I needed to protect my hard-won sanity. I left her shouting into a vacuum.

Ongoing rage comes at a high price. I think that forgiveness is the most important idea that the story of Jesus introduced into our dialogue, and some form of forgiveness needs to be part of the healing process. Without it, moving ahead may be impossible. In her novel, *The Zenith*, exiled Vietnamese writer Duong Thu Huong has a character say, "Everything depends on the compassion of the living. Only compassion can open our minds, enlighten us to what is needed."

Forgiveness is complicated.

The night he let me hit him, I had to accept the truth of his vulnerability. Usually it was hidden by his dogma-defending rage. I think my father's public life involved playing a role that required deep denial based on the faith that he would be forgiven by his God. It allowed him to bury deep the part of himself he needed to have forgiven. On the night he let me hit him, I had called him out, and in that moment the guilt he carried overwhelmed him.

Kate's memory adds a dimension to his character that throws everything I understood about him out of focus. That night he exposed himself to me as broken, but I can no longer believe his sense of failure was only about me. When I confronted him, the shell cracked, but his guilt about Kate had probably created a weak spot.

Accepting his vulnerability as an integral part of him opened the door for me to settle my account with him. I hit him back and it defined every interaction I had with him afterward. The exchange left me without a father's guidance, but it also opened a path to sanity. I was freed to find my own means to embrace life with all its complexity and obligations. I was lucky. I was able to form other supportive relationships, connecting with people who saw better things in me than I saw in myself.

Kate has since told me that she went to see him in the nursing home. When she confronted him, he was certifiably insane. Rather than own up, he deflected to the Lord, tried to get Kate to pray. When he died, her path to peace became more obfuscated. Had our father been more coherent when she voiced her accusation, it might have been different for both of them.

Eugenia Collier's observation about memory in her story, "Marigolds"—that it's an abstract painting and presents things as they feel, rather than as they are—rings true to me. I don't know the details of Kate's experiences with my father, but I am convinced that she encountered a much darker place in his psyche than I did.

I wish I'd been able to offer her more help than I did.

At his memorial service in Thurmond Auditorium at Ascension Ministries, the memory of my father as a servant of God was honored as though he were an example of someone to be looked up to for his dedication to his faith.

Kate did not attend.

Twenty-seven

My son-in-law has a small construction company. He's black and
was sharing his frustration with me about a white general contractor he had done some work for and who had refused to pay
the expense of contractually covered changes in the project. Un-
foreseen complications added unplanned excavator and dump
truck time. The proper change-order notifications had been sub-
mitted. The contractor was trying to stiff him. My son-in-law
knows his business well. He had kept his cool and it had taken a
year of living with cash flow problems, but through patience and
working the proper channels, he'd finally gotten paid.

I'm deeply impressed by his ability to elude rage, not just in
his work, but in general. To survive and succeed, he has to stay
calm and handle situations daily that would cause me to lose my
temper and lash out. I asked him how he does it. He said that
instead of getting caught up in blame, or retaliation, he tries to
find a way to move forward. He tries to identify the immediate
problem and solve it. He's one of the healthiest people I know.

In Hoi An, a town on the Thu Bôn River south of Da Nang, we
spent the afternoon exploring between the hotel and the river.
The area included shops, many spilling into the street, restau-
rants, and a covered market with stalls selling fresh fish, shrimp
and eels, fruit and vegetables, shoes, clothing, and almost anything else you can imagine.

The daypack I used on the trip was new and exactly like one
I had been using for years. I'd received both of them as an in-

ducement to donate money to a charitable cause. My new pack
fell apart at LAX, and I found a temporary way to make it work
but was looking to replace it. I had been warned that anything I
bought with an American brand name would be a knock-off, but
that didn't matter to me as long as it was affordable and worked.
A display of luggage at one of the open-air street shops included a small Mountain Gear backpack that met my need. The girl
tending the stall used a pole with a hook to get it down and we
settled on a price.

At the beautiful open-air restaurant by the river where we
were having lunch, I transferred some of my stuff and scrunched
the old pack still partially loaded inside the new one. Back at the
hotel, I needed something from the new pack and discovered the
zipper to the compartment where I had put important papers,
like airline ticket numbers to get home, was stuck. Our tour guide
saw me struggling and said I should return to the shop and exchange the pack. Johnny assured me it would work.

I hadn't been paying close attention to where we were and
wasn't sure I could find the shop again, but on a map we narrowed the likelihood to an area close enough that Johnny thought
I could make it back in time. I didn't want to miss the boat tour
of the river.

I had to dodge aggressive street vendors as I looked for familiar landmarks, keeping close track of time. I found the shop
and the girl recognized me. Our interaction had the familiarity of
working with non-English speaking students in my high school
classes. When she understood, she immediately offered an exchange. Seeing that I needed the stuff from the broken pack, she
went to work on the zipper. I pointed to my watch and made a
desperate face. I either had to head back soon or miss the boat
trip.

She motioned and I followed her into the crowded but tidy
living space behind the shop where a man and woman at least a

generation younger than me and who must have been the girl's parents greeted me and invited me to sit down at the table. They seemed comfortable with me. The feeling was surprisingly warm, and I wondered if they would offer tea when the zipper problem was fixed. A transaction involving a similar level of respect and kindness could never happen at Target or Walmart. It dawned on me that the site of the My Lai massacre was not far from there.

I tried to communicate that I was in a hurry without disrespecting them. Needle-nose pliers and an ice pick finally achieved zipper movement, and the man deftly worked the pull until he got it to slide freely. He handed the pack to me and I transferred the contents into the new one. Standing, I held the old pack upside down, all compartments open, above the table and watched forgotten American change I'd purged from my pants pockets spill out. They rushed to help me gather the coins from the floor. I tried to let them know how thankful I was before I looked at my watch and hurried back to the street.

It was rush hour and everything looked different. I felt lost and was afraid I would miss the boat excursion. At an intersection I hoped was near the hotel, a small opening appeared in an impenetrable wall of traffic. I'd seen it done here, so I stepped out and it worked. The vehicular sea parted enough for me to cross, and when I found the hotel, the tour group was waiting in front. I held up the new pack and they cheered.

When I think of the girl and the family in the shop where I exchanged my backpack, I have a hard time relating to the word *gook*, or grasping what happened at My Lai.

Time and new experience have caused my memories of my father to lose power. I've lived a third of my life since his passing, watching blood counts, fighting something physical and intimately personal.

Since our father's death, Kate has had her ups and downs,

but she seems to have found a way to live her life. Her kids have grown into adults we're all proud of. She has worked in hostels and been great with her grandkids. Kate and I are not close, but we're not enemies either.

When I think of the possibilities life offers, the connection I've shared with my own kids, for me, my father's legacy is mostly grief for what might have been but wasn't.

Twenty-eight

The lean-to on the back of the barn is falling down. The barn's hand-split cedar shake roof has been replaced with corrugated metal, and you can hear more noise from the airport industrial park between here and the interstate, but the blackberry vines are still thick and the air still smells like mountain woods. A Safeway and a McDonald's are down on the flat less than two miles away, along with the new elementary school, medical center, apartment buildings, and subdivisions for Boeing workers that crowd up to the base of the bluff.

I'll cut a few trees from a stand of alders that borders the back pasture, limb them, drag the limbs back into the woods to rot, then cut the logs into rounds to take home and split for stove wood. To get my pickup there, I need to open a makeshift gate and take down a section of the fence. The cows are foraging out of sight, and I don't think I need to isolate them.

As I approach the barbed wire strand that surrounds the weathered shed, I hear the familiar pulse of the electric transformer sending out its current. He made fences with a single strand of electrified barbed wire strung between insulators on trees or metal stakes. Though erected decades ago as temporary, they're still functional. The gates are just places in the charged wire that can be disconnected, a hook with a plastic handle that keeps you from getting shocked only if everything is dry. A charged wire at crotch level isolates a manure-free zone around the pump house and well area, and there's no gate. Stepping over is risky, especially with shoes wet from the night's rainfall.

When I open the pump house door, I'm hit by the stale, close
air, the smell of musty wood, wet concrete and rusting pipes. A
big spider scurries into a crack as I brush away cobwebs and pull
the plug on the transformer. As the charger's pulsing stops, the
pump comes on. The needle on the gauge moves as the pressure
builds, and I wait to hear the comforting click of the relay that
shuts the pump off at the end of the cycle. Behind a grove of trees
and out of sight, there are renters in his house. The well, though
shallow enough to have run dry a few times during late-summer
hot spells, has provided good water.

Outside, I notice a slug climbing the damp side of the mossed-
over cement well casing. The slug is big and brown and looks
like something you wouldn't want to step in. The casing is sealed
and it is as unlikely today that the slug can get in as it was when
he still lived here and phoned, saying he wouldn't drink the water. But he couldn't explain what the problem was, so I came. I
thought it might be mechanical and therefore neutral, part of the
common ground we had cultivated between the fences we had
built, fences separating the huge parts of our lives that couldn't
overlap. We had learned to keep the manure out of the well and
we were careful not to dig into the hardpan.

On that day I checked the pump, and, like today, it was cycling
fine. When I understood that he was saying there were slugs in
the water, I had to accept that his wife had not been wrong when
she complained about him wasting money buying two new electric fence chargers. The one I just unplugged is one of them.

I have two trees down and have the undercut notched in this one.
I'm close to the critical point in the uppercut, the cut in the backside of the trunk. It's a big tree, and maybe an inch of wood pre-
vents the beginning of motion and the cracking sound that will
signal its fall.

Something makes me look up.

Here come the cows.

There are eight of them, steers actually. They're ignorant of the danger, tame, curious, and bored. They'll mouth the alder leaves for the new taste, and they're gathering where the tree will fall. Some of them belong to David, my youngest brother, who bought five acres of my father's land and lives here. The steers graze on both properties. Part of one of my brother's steers will end up in my freezer, but I'd rather the hired hit man from the beef-packing house down on the flat had the job than end up with the picture that instantly forms in my mind when I see them in the path of the tree. The rest of the herd are boarders and don't belong to us, which makes it even worse.

I kill the saw and set it down.

I don't like the idea of going into the fall zone with the tree about ready to let go, but there they stand looking as stupid as I feel.

I yell.

They stare.

I brave the tree and run at them, yelling and waving a branch.

They clear the area for a moment, but return to the leaves when I head for the saw.

I think fast and decide to hurt them enough to maybe make them hesitate before they return. I throw firewood sticks, hitting some of them. They bellow and run. I keep chasing and throwing until I think they're far enough away and traumatized enough to stay put for a while.

It works.

I start the saw and soon the tree comes crashing down.

My father has been dead for years, but I'm using his saw, axes he gave me, and skill I learned from him. He's gone from here, but it's still his haunt, with his fences. His handprints are all over it and me. Before I head home, I drag the brush from the pasture and restring the wire at the edge of the woods. I check on the cows, secure all the gates, and return to the pump house to plug in the fence charger.

For now anyway, there's water in the well, the pump is working, and the beasts are in their proper places.

Epilogue

My body's ongoing battle to suppress the leukemia was successful for twenty years. For fifteen years after my second treatment,
key blood counts had bounced around, staying below normal
but in a range that was working. When I had counts that were
dangerously low, they always came back up enough that I had a
working immune system, and certain red flags on the lab report
lost their power to shake my world. Even though I worked in a
classroom, exposed to everything that came by, I rarely got sick.
I had gotten used to uncertainty, to limbo, to holding the appre-
hension at bay.

During my last years of teaching, the counts had risen to alert-
free ranges and stabilized. Along with my doctors, I started to
think of the cancer as something I had gotten past. Allie and I had
started reading brochures, trying to decide where to go for our
fortieth-anniversary trip. The money was in a special account.

As I was paddling my kayak along the beach north of our
house, my stomach started to cramp. I managed to make it home,
got the kayak put away and got up to the house before the pain
became debilitating. The emergency room team found a kidney
stone blocking the tube to the bladder. In the process of getting it
fixed, I learned there were several more stones lurking. The next
one struck when I was in the pool with my grandson at his swim-
ming lesson. We put off the trip until I was declared stone-free.
When that happened we settled on Vietnam as a destination.

While we were planning the trip, I kept following my normal
cancer-check routine. When the blood counts took a dip, I didn't

panic. I had no new symptoms. I hoped the dip was just a phase, a bump in the road. Oncology visits had lost their intensity. My new doctor was young. I wasn't his crisis of the day. My disease was now considered highly treatable and probably was already designated so when he was in medical school. He would read my lab report, poke my spleen, tell me I was doing fine and send me on my way. He didn't seem to take my case as seriously as did the two doctors, now retired, who had been there for my earlier treatment.

The oncology clinic has changed too. It has expanded and is now on the ground floor of a new, modern building across the street from the hospital. It has its own lab off the comfortable waiting room. The blood draw is a brief, usually painless interruption before the nurse comes for you. For my twenty or thirty anxious minutes sitting among the other patients, some in wheel chairs, many wearing wigs or hats, I would wait for confirmation that I'd escaped and was no longer one of them. The sense of relief as I passed through again on my way out was always overwhelming.

My doctor surprised me by scheduling a bone marrow biopsy. He made the case that it had been twenty years, and it was time to create a new baseline and document what was going on inside me. I resisted. I didn't want to become a cancer patient again. We did the biopsy anyway. He was really good at taking the sample. It wasn't much worse than a flu shot. I learned that twenty percent of the cells my marrow was making were cancerous. The new biopsy cut through my insulation, removed my sense of distance from the patients in the waiting room.

The biopsy result wasn't good news, but not bad enough to do anything. It was possible that it would remain stable indefinitely. Since I seemed to be managing well enough with no real symptoms, we got shots and visas and went on the Vietnam adventure. Jet lag and irregular sleep didn't seem to affect me more than anyone else. I felt okay.

After the trip, spring yard work required frequent rest breaks and I seemed to be out of breath more than usual. Sometimes I got dizzy. A scrape on my shin from splitting firewood didn't seem to be infected, but it got worse instead of better. I'm not young anymore, and early symptoms are pretty subtle. I really didn't want to be a cancer patient again. I tried to ignore it. My annual physical exam with my primary care doctor was due. A blood count check is also part of that routine, and I learned the counts had taken a serious dive. I went back to the oncologist who confirmed that we were at the place where it was time to treat. The other shoe was dropping.

During the first several years of the remission, with my blood counts bouncing around and the probability of having to do battle again always looming, I wasn't sure I had the will or the strength to survive. Now that treatment was imminent, the memories came flooding back.

The chemo drugs themselves are only part of the challenge. It takes a cocktail of other drugs to help your body accommodate and survive the chemo. They give you drugs to help process the massive cell kill, to avoid allergic reactions, to combat nausea, to cover for your lack of an immune system. Both past treatments had required blood transfusions. After the first cladribine treatment, they sent me home and by the end of the day I was back in the hospital with hives and a high fever. They were trying to keep me alive, and there was no way of knowing which drug or combination had caused the reaction.

Here we go again!

Hairy cell leukemia is now considered treatable in most cases and the drug, cladribine, is still a frontline treatment. But after two treatments, it's recommended that something different be tried. Because of my history, my oncologist sent me to Seattle Cancer Care Alliance to have my case appraised by one of their research doctors to see if there were any clinical trials or new treatments and to determine the best strategy.

People come from all over the country for treatment at Seattle Cancer Care Alliance. It's where the hard cases get sent. Being referred there was a relief, but it still felt pretty ominous. At least I would be getting cutting-edge care by people who were at the forefront of research into my disease. I got a call from a woman who welcomed me to the treatment program. She said she would be my facilitator. Since my first appointment was early in the morning, my wife and I spent the night at the hostel for patients and their caregivers near the clinic.

The hostel rooms could be rented by the month, week or night. Our room, like all of them, was designed to be easily sterilized. It was comfortable and practical with a refrigerator and kitchenette. Surfaces were hard plastic, mostly white, and the furniture was simple and disinfectant friendly. We envisioned spending nights before early appointments or after infusions when I would be too sick for the drive home. The clerk who checked us in had lived in our town and had gone to our high school, but hadn't taken any of my classes. It would be manageable and we would get through it.

In the morning, the clinic was crowded. It had the same heavy-traffic, bustling-city feel as downtown. But people were nice. Everyone there was either a cancer patient or a support for one and there was a feeling in the air, both of the gravity of it all and of understanding and compassion. The clinic staff did a good job of easing the inherent anxiety overshadowing the sense of commotion. We waited in line to get registered, then found our way to our doctor's office. Our wait there was short.

The doctor was interested in the story of my past treatment. He was an instructor at the University of Washington School of Medicine, doing research on ways to engage the immune system to recognize and kill cancer. He agreed to take on my case. We would begin treatment right away with infusions of pentostatin and rituximab. We were told the chance of achieving remission with this combination was ninety percent. This was very reassuring, but I'd been there before and knew it all hinged on how my body would react. Overall, we were relieved and felt like we were in good hands. These people knew what they were doing, and if there were complications, this would be the place to have them.

So when I got the phone call from our medical insurance company saying the request for transfer of care from the local cancer care center to Seattle Cancer Care Alliance was denied, we were devastated. I was sure there was a mistake and got on the phone. Everyone was polite and cooperative. The Seattle doctor even called personally to explain and apologize, but treatment in Seattle didn't offer any clear, documentable advantage that would change the insurance company's decision. The prescribed drugs weren't that new and could be administered at the local clinic for less money. The Seattle appointments were cancelled and new ones set up at the local infusion center.

The evening we learned of the insurance company's decision, we were having dinner with a couple who lives near us, both doctors. They have a high opinion of my local oncologist and assured us I would get excellent treatment. I wouldn't have the inconvenience of driving to Seattle, especially if something unexpected happened. I soon found out they were right.

A PIC tube was put in my right arm and I was ready to start. This time I'd be an outpatient. The routine would be infusions every other Monday. The Monday between would be the nadir, or low point. Until my reaction stabilized and it was clear that I was handling the drugs, I would also go in then for a blood draw to see what was happening. The second week of the cycle would be recovery time, getting ready for the next round.

Both the Seattle doctor and my local oncologist had prescribed allopurinal, a gout medicine, to help my body deal with the cell

kill from the chemo drugs. I started taking it before the first infusion appointment and immediately had an allergic reaction.
Hives broke out all over my body, head to foot. I tested my local
clinic's system for dealing with off-hours emergencies. It worked.
I got the answering service on the phone and a doctor called back
within minutes. I told him my symptoms. He said I should stop
the drug, called in a prescription for steroids, and sent me to a
pharmacy. He also reassured me that there were other ways to
deal with the cell-kill problem.

I'd never been to the new Infusion Center. It's down a hallway beyond the examining rooms and the doctors' private offices. You're greeted by coffee and tea set up on one side of the
entry, and a counter opposite with fresh fruit, snacks and a large
stainless kettle of hot soup. My first thought was, *Food at a chemo
center? Who's going to eat that?* There was a volunteer greeter who
gave us a cancer-care welcome bag with a fleece blanket, water,
writing tablet and pen, a game, and hand sanitizer. I'm officially
a cancer patient again.

The Infusion Center is spacious, much different from the little three-chair alcove in the hospital across the street I went to
twenty years ago. Fifteen matching gray recliners line the glassed
exterior wall. There are also private rooms. Each station has an IV
stand on wheels with a digital pump. On busy days all stations
are occupied. Mondays are always busy. Across the aisle, counter
space is covered with thick, neatly arranged files, each accompanied by a red plastic fishing-tackle type of box used to convey today's drug cocktail. The cabinets beneath the counter are stocked
with sterile kits packaged for specific procedures such as access-
ing a patient's port, or changing a PIC line dressing.

Outside the glass wall there's a courtyard garden that I've only
caught glimpses of on my way to a station. All the recliners I've
been assigned have faced away from it, but it gives you a sense
of peace and safety that would be absent if the windows looked

out on the street. Like me, most patients are accompanied by a caregiver. Wi-Fi is free. The patients read, use a device, or doze, depending on how the infusion is affecting them. There are lots of head scarves here. Lots of pale, sick-looking people and half a dozen nurses, tending us. Allie usually passes the time reading.

When they deliver two cases of Ensure to the guy next to me, I flash back to the hospital stays when it was the only nutrient I could force down. The nurse would bring a large paper cup with crushed ice and pour in two cans of chocolate Ensure. It took some mental preparation before I would try to down it and only once did it come back up, all over the nurse who was standing by.

We're at the moment of truth. The nurse, who is all business, projects competence but also breaks through with an occasional smile or remark that lets you know she's human and gets what you're going through. Today I get a small dose of rituximab to see how it goes. I'll also get Benadryl and something to settle my stomach. I've taken the anti-nausea drug in pill form. We're being careful, testing each step. They start out by dripping it in slowly, upping the rate every twenty-five minutes, checking my vitals. The first half-hour is uneventful.

The headache hits suddenly, followed closely by nausea. I signal Allie who gets the attention of the nurse. They stop the infusion and I have the panicky thought that this could mean I can't go through the treatment. Someone reports to the doctor. We wait. The doctor's instructions arrive. Add steroids and keep it slow. It works, no more headaches or nausea. They follow with a liter of saline to hydrate and purge. I return each of the two following days for hydration.

Over the following weeks each support drug is tested separately, in low dosage. When there is no bad reaction, dosage is gradually increased. Then, both chemo drugs are tried on the same day, and eventually I am able to settle into a two-week cycle, getting full doses of all the drugs without an adverse reaction.

Gradually my blood counts improve. The off-week blood test is discontinued. There are more hives and dizzy spells, triggering off-hours calls to the answering service, a trip to the emergency room for atrial fibrillation, visits to a cardiologist, spleen ultrasounds. It isn't all smooth sailing, but I don't lose my hair, and am able to go home after chemo sessions and eat!

After five months I am sent home, my blood free of mutant cells and my spleen back to normal size. It takes a few more months and some other drugs before I actually start feeling healthy, but it's spring again and I don't get dizzy or out of breath doing yard work.

Another extension!

My friend Ben is right, no one gets out of here alive, so I'm leaving for a Greek vacation the day after tomorrow.

"What's the point of tiptoeing through life to end up safely on death's door?"

—Attributed to Ludicris

Wayne M. Johnston taught English, Creative Writing and Publications at La Conner High School for nineteen years. For twenty-two years prior to teaching, he worked on tugboats, usually as chief engineer, towing freight barges between Canadian and West Coast ports. In 2011, he won the *Soundings Review* First Publication Award for his essay, "Sailing."

He lives with his wife, Sally, on Fidalgo Island in Washington State where he continues to write.